Dear Reader,

Ideas for books come from everywhere. The idea for this book actually came from personal experience. Anyone who knows me knows I have no sense of direction. I can get turned around in a huge discount store and have to stop and ask someone how to find the exit! I have taken many a detour in my travels, some of which have led to meeting interesting people and discovering beautiful faces. (Of course, some of them also lead to lots of frustration.)

My husband, a man who was born with an internal compass, is amazed at how easily I get lost, but he's learned to live with it. I've long wanted to write about a directionally challenged woman and an always-knows-where-he's-headed man who learn to love each other. So here it is. I hope you enjoy Marlee and Craig's story.

And if you ever see me driving aimlessly down a street near you, take pity and offer to give me directions!

Cindi Myers

P.S. I love to hear from readers. Write me at P.O. Box 991, Bailey, CO 80421 or e-mail Cindi@CindiMyers.com. Visit me on the Web at www.CindiMyers.com.

Take deep breaths.
There's no need to panic.

Marlee gripped the steering wheel so tightly her fingers were pratically fused to the leather. She gnawed her lower lip and tried to think calming thoughts.

Except that she didn't have a clue where she was, or even if she was headed in the right direction. She glanced over at Craig, still sleeping, snoring softly. Thank God he wasn't awake to witness this.

She'd done fine for the first hour or so driving. Then one of those nasty orange signs had popped up on the side of the road. *Detour*.

She'd told herself she could handle it, she just had to follow the signs. No problem.

Except she must have missed one of the signs, or maybe they'd forgotten to put one out. By that point she'd made two or three turns and had been completely confused.

So she'd guessed. A dangerous proposition, but the only other alternative was to wake Craig. And admit that she'd gotten lost. In the middle of nowhere. Not anywhere close to his precious planned route.

And what self-respecting woman wanted to do that?

Detour Ahead

Cindi Myers

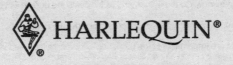

HARLEQUIN®

TORONTO • NEW YORK • LONDON
AMSTERDAM • PARIS • SYDNEY • HAMBURG
STOCKHOLM • ATHENS • TOKYO • MILAN • MADRID
PRAGUE • WARSAW • BUDAPEST • AUCKLAND

ISBN 0-373-44209-2

DETOUR AHEAD

Copyright © 2005 by Cynthia Myers.

This edition published by arrangement with Harlequin Books S.A.

® and TM are trademarks of the publisher. Trademarks indicated with ® are registered in the United States Patent and Trademark Office, the Canadian Trade Marks Office and in other countries.

www.eHarlequin.com

Printed in U.S.A.

ABOUT THE AUTHOR

Cindi Myers believes in love at first sight, good chocolate, cold champagne, that people who don't like animals can't be trusted and that God obviously has a sense of humor. She also believes in writing fun, sexy romances about people she hopes readers will fall in love with. In addition to writing, Cindi enjoys reading, quilting, gardening, hiking and downhill skiing. She lives in the Rocky Mountains of Colorado with her husband (whom she met on a blind date and agreed to marry six weeks later) and two spoiled dogs.

Books by Cindi Myers

Don't miss any of our special offers. Write to us at the following address for information on our newest releases.

Harlequin Reader Service
U.S.: 3010 Walden Ave., P.O. Box 1325, Buffalo, NY 14269
Canadian: P.O. Box 609, Fort Erie, Ont. L2A 5X3

1

THOSE OF YOU who've been following this Web diary for a while know that I am somewhat directionally impaired. In fact, you may recall I began this blog as a way of sharing some of my more interesting adventures while deviating from my original route— in other words, crazy things that happened to me while getting lost.

But my latest attempt to find my way in unfamiliar surroundings has landed me in hot water. I'm almost embarrassed to admit it here, but then, when have I ever held anything back from you, my faithful readers?

I lost my license.

I don't mean I've misplaced the thing and can't find it. I mean it was taken away from me. Pulled. I'm no longer a legal driver.

I was driving the wrong way down a one-way street and... And the traffic court judge took one look at the points on my driving record and confiscated my license. It wouldn't have been so bad if I hadn't racked up all those speeding tickets, too. And if I hadn't been cited two other times for carelessness behind the wheel. Can I help it if I make a few wrong turns sometimes?

Maybe it's like my friend Susan says. I need to

> *carry a compass. Of course, then I'd have to learn to*
> *actually read a compass. A Girl Scout I was not....*
>   *Just thought I'd share that update. Now, real life*
> *beckons.*

Real life in the form of two projects that needed to be finished by Friday, four phone calls to return and a handful of mail to open. Not to mention Susan's wedding to deal with. Marlee Jones sighed and signed off from her *Travels with Marlee* Web site. What had begun as a way to teach herself HTML code had turned into a guilty pleasure. Her Web log, or blog, pulled in several hundred hits a day and she actually got fan mail. Most of it from nice ordinary people. Of course there was Dave, who wrote to her from Cellblock Sixteen at the state pen, but he at least was polite, and safely locked away for life, or so her contact in the criminal justice department had assured her.

She shook her head and picked up the heavy cream-colored envelope she kept propped against her monitor.

> Mr. and Mrs. Anthony St. John request that you
> join them in celebrating the marriage of their
> daughter, Susan Elisabeth, to Bryan Fredericks,
> son of Mr. and Mrs. Wayne Fredericks and
> Alison Reynolds.

Susan would have a fit when Marlee told her the latest. She ought to be calling any second now....

The phone rang and Marlee picked it up on the second ring. "Hello, Susan."

"How did you know it was me?"

"I'm psychic."

"No, really, how did you know? Did your cheap-ass boss finally spring for caller ID?"

"Gary isn't cheap, he's frugal. After all, we are a nonprofit organization."

"That's his excuse for everything. But I notice that *he* isn't doing without the finer things in life, while you labor away in that little closet of an office."

Marlee glanced around her office, which had, in fact, been a storage closet in another life. Yeah, it was small and dingy and out of the way, but that had its advantages. Nobody ever bothered her back here and she was pretty much free to do what she liked.

"You're not answering my question," Susan said. "Since when are you psychic?"

"I know you've got *Travels with Marlee* linked to your home page. You read the new post, didn't you?"

"What's this about losing your license? How does a grown woman lose her license?"

"It's not my fault," Marlee protested. "Some people are born without a sense of direction. There've been studies."

"You're a study all right. The big question is, how are you going to get to my wedding? Don't think I'm going to go through this without you. Besides, there's a groomsman I want you to meet."

"Susan!" Marlee rolled her eyes. Though Susan fancied herself a matchmaker, the truth was, her fix-ups always ended up broken. "I'm coming to be with you at your wedding, not to meet a man."

"But this one would be perfect for you."

"Right. Like that accordion player—what was his name, Terry?"

"Larry. And I thought you'd appreciate his quirkiness."

"He was a *horrible* accordion player. And his idea

of a hot date was a visit to the Air and Space Museum, to look at *every single* exhibit."

"So I was a little off with that one. This guy I know you'll like. But first you have to get here to meet him. Without a driver's license, how are you going to do that? I know you won't fly."

Marlee shuddered. Looking at all those planes at the museum had been bad enough—no way was she getting on one. "Maybe I could take a bus." She glanced over at the computer on her credenza. A chorus line of chimpanzees tap-danced their way across the monitor screen. Could she look up bus schedules online?

"Ick. It would take a week. You'd be a wreck by the time you got here. I don't want my maid of honor looking like she slept sitting up for a week."

Marlee sighed. She didn't particularly want to try sleeping sitting up. Now that she was on the downhill slide toward thirty, even a couple of nights of less than blissful slumber made fine lines and dark circles appear out of nowhere. "What about the train?"

"Hello? Have you ever checked an Amtrak schedule? To get from D.C. to San Diego you have to change trains umpteen times and it takes like four days. It would be as bad as the bus. And way more expensive."

"I guess I could try to catch a ride with someone else. Any other guests driving from D.C. to San Diego for the wedding?" Susan and Bryan had met in the capital city, so it stood to reason other wedding guests were from here. Though most of them were probably flying. Let them trust their lives to a heavy metal tube floating on air. She'd stay firmly on the ground, thank you very much.

"That's a brilliant idea!" Susan sounded thrilled.

"It is?" As ideas went, it didn't sound particularly spectacular to Marlee. She spent every day design-ing wildly creative ads for non-profits. Using rappers to promote the Reading Is Fundamental program—now *that* was a brilliant idea, but this...?

"Craig Brinkman is driving from D.C. You can ride with him."

"Uh-huh. Who is Craig Brinkman?" She picked up a pencil and wrote a note for herself to call the metro library about a photo shoot.

"He's Bryan's old college roommate. The best man, as a matter of fact. It's the perfect solution."

"This isn't the guy you're trying to fix me up with, is it? Because I really don't want to be fixed up right now." Or ever, if Susan was doing the fixing. She was a great friend, but she didn't have a clue what Mar-lee really wanted in a man. But then, Marlee wasn't too sure on that score either.

"Craig?" Susan's laugh came out more like a snort. "Absolutely not. Craig Brinkman is definitely not your type."

"Why do you say that? If he's so awful, why are you suggesting I travel all the way across the coun-try with him?"

"He's not awful. In fact, he's a really nice guy. But he's sort of uptight. A real overachiever."

Marlee looked around her closet office. "And I'm an underachiever." *Ouch.*

"You're just not as ambitious as Craig. I mean, this is the man with a plan—for everything."

She made a face. Craig Brinkman definitely didn't sound like her type of guy. And not someone she wanted to spend a week in close quarters with. With her laid-back approach to life, she'd have him driv-ing off a cliff inside of two days. Three, tops. "I don't know, Suz. Drive cross-country with a man I've never even met? It seems kind of weird."

"Craig's a nice guy, really. One thing about being anal, he won't get lost. And he's one of Bryan's oldest friends. You like Bryan, don't you?"

As if I'd be clueless enough to tell you if I didn't like the man you're going to marry. But thankfully, she didn't have to fake liking Bryan Fredericks. He was a genuinely good guy. Chances were this friend of his was a good guy too. Still…

"Craig will probably appreciate the company," Susan continued. "And you can split expenses. I'll have Bryan call him and set it all up."

Marlee chewed her lower lip. If she was going to make Susan's wedding, it was either gut it up to get on a plane, or accept a ride with mysterious Craig. "Okay. And thanks. I dreaded the thought of having to miss your wedding."

"No way are you going to miss this. How many other best friends do you think I have? It's too late to order another dress—or to find another gal pal."

Marlee laughed. "Thanks. I can't wait to see you again."

"I can't wait to see you. I need you here to help me deal with all the wedding craziness."

"That bad, huh?"

"You try interviewing six caterers and three florists in one week. It's enough to make me want to elope."

"Then why don't you?"

"I said I was crazy, not insane. I've waited years for my dream wedding and I won't let anything stop me from having it. Including a maid of honor with no sense of direction."

"Right, well, have this Craig guy give me a call.

We'll see if we can't work something out." She hung up the phone and relaxed in her chair, bouncing against the springy back. Susan sounded so happy. So in love. The tiniest pinch of jealousy grabbed hold of Marlee. Why did some women find love so easily while others never seemed to get a break?

She herself had had about as much luck finding Mr. Right as she did finding her way around the city in traffic. Maybe whatever genetic flaw led to her always getting lost was connected to her inability to sustain a relationship. Sure, she had plenty of male friends, but not one special man. Men didn't take her seriously. Her last boyfriend had flat-out told her he couldn't plan a future with a woman who didn't even think about lunch ahead of time.

So what was wrong with being spontaneous? Her motto was Be Prepared—for Anything!

She sat straight in her chair again and resolutely opened the file for RIF. Was her carefree attitude a sign of immaturity? After all, what kind of grown woman lost her license? And while all her friends had moved on to high-profile jobs and fancy homes and families of their own, she still lived in a funky little carriage-house apartment in Georgetown, and had a job that provided more satisfaction than salary. No wonder men looking to settle down steered clear of her.

She let out another sigh and told herself to concentrate on work. Marching along to a set plan for her life sounded like sheer drudgery. She couldn't see living in a certain kind of house or working a certain kind of job just because it was expected. She needed more freedom to move around, to go with the flow.

If that made her man-poison, so be it. Except for

her lackluster love life, she was happy, and what more could a girl ask for?

Except maybe a better internal compass.

FROM: TopToque@govnet.net
To: Marlee@TWM.com
Subject: Driving to San Diego
Understand you need ride to Bry & Suz's wedding. Am leaving Sat. June 6, 8 a.m. sharp. You're welcome if you can pay your expenses. Expect 5 nights on road. Let me know ASAP.

Marlee frowned at the e-mail message that showed up in her box two days after her conversation with Susan. She assumed this "TopToque" character was Craig Brinkman. He wasn't much on small talk, was he? A little "Hello, how are you, my name's Craig," wouldn't have been out of line, would it?

Okay, maybe she was being too hard on the guy. Maybe he was shy. Or he felt awkward about this whole give-a-ride-to-a-stranger thing. She could relate to that.

No problem, then. She'd be the one to break the ice. She'd show him how it was done.

From: Marlee@TWM.com
To: TopToque@govnet.net
Subject: Road Trip!
Hi Craig. Good to hear from you. I'm Marlee Jones, erstwhile best woman in need of a ride to San Diego. Thanks so much for agreeing to help me out here. I promise I'll be good company and, of course, I'll pay my share of the costs.

Since we're going to be spending some time together on the road, I thought it might be nice to get to know each other a little first. How about coffee or a drink sometime? Call me at 555-6129. I'm looking forward to meeting you!
Marlee

Smiling to herself, she hit the Send button. That should thaw Craig out a little. They could meet for a drink, hammer out the details of the trip and when it was time to hit the road they'd practically be old friends instead of strangers.

"Hey, Marl." Gretchen Wunderlich, her boss Gary's secretary, slipped into Marlee's closet/office. "Gary told me to give these to you." She dumped a pile of multi-colored papers on Marlee's desk.

"What is all this?" She frowned at the top sheet, "Sterilization Techniques for Meat Handlers."

"P.I.O. sheets that need to be updated. Gary says to work on them as you get the chance."

Public Information Office sheets always needed updating. Most of them dated from the forties and fifties. Marlee pulled a pale-pink sheet of paper from the stack. "Safe Food Handling for the Housewife" was illustrated with drawings of a smiling woman in a full-skirted dress, apron and high heels. "Why did Gary send these to me?" she asked.

Gretchen leaned against the doorjamb and smacked a wad of gum the color of a honeydew melon. "They've been cluttering up the office for months now. I got tired of moving them around and complained, so Gary had me bring them here."

"So now they can clutter up my office. Gee, thanks." She frowned at the six-inch high tower of paper. "I thought the interns were supposed to do this kind of grunt work." As a nonprofit, the agency relied on interns from George Washington University for free labor.

"This semester's intern is designing an animation program for the art department."

Great. Now even the interns did more exciting work than Marlee. "Tell Gary I don't think I'll be able to get to this anytime soon."

"No prob." Gretchen heaved herself upright once more and started to leave. She stopped halfway out the door and swung around to face Marlee again. "I almost forgot—Gary really liked your idea to use the rappers for the Reading Is Fundamental promo."

"Great." Of course, it would have been greater if Gary had managed to tell her this himself, but she'd learned to be grateful for small favors.

Gretchen was almost out the door again when Marlee stopped her. "Gary knows about my vacation, right? Remind him I'll be away the next two weeks."

"I'll remind him. Knowing Gary, he won't even notice you're gone." Gretchen waved over her shoulder, then was gone, her feet slapping on the tile floor in rhythm with her popping gum.

Marlee sank into her chair and stared at the P.I.O. sheets. So much for the artistic, interesting and important work she always bragged about whenever her friends asked why she continued to work for a peanuts-for-pay nonprofit when she could be plying her trade for real dough at one of the big ad firms around town.

Not that she hadn't asked herself from time to time if she was really making the best use of her talents. Sure, working for programs like Reading Is

Fundamental and the March of Dimes was rewarding and important, but was she selling herself short by not being more ambitious?

Ambition sounded like so much hard work. She'd always been one to go with the flow and see where life took her next. Only lately she felt as if the flow had stopped and she wasn't going much of anywhere.

She shoved the P.I.O. busywork aside and opened a new file on her computer. Writing new blog entries always helped her to sort out her thoughts.

Road trip!

Don't those words immediately make you think of fun and adventure? Whether it's a Spring Break caravan to the Florida beaches or a summer safari across the country, hitting the road with friends for a few days away from the grind is a sure cure for a case of the dulls.

Yours truly is about to set off on a cross-country odyssey of my own. I'll be traveling from D.C. to San Diego to attend by best gal pal Susan's wedding.

Before you start alerting state police to be on the lookout for me, rest assured that I will not be driving myself on this trip. (See previous entry for the whole sad story of my recently departed driver's license.) No, I have the privilege of a chauffeur for this vacation, the wedding best man. More on him later.

Right now I'm musing about the value of road trips in general and this one in particular. I'm thinking this will be the perfect time to take a closer look at where I'm headed—literally and figuratively.

Don't worry, though, I don't intend to get too serious. I'm not forgetting this is a vacation, too. And vacations are for fun. For cutting loose and doing things we might not do in the confines of our ordi-

nary lives. How else to explain the penchant for Las Vegas conventioneers to sing karaoke or overly pale beachgoers to throw their backs out doing the limbo?

So expect a few surprises from yours truly in the coming weeks. Though I don't know exactly how yet, I intend to find my own way to cut loose.

MARLEE was well into her regular Wednesday-night movie marathon when the phone rang. She was tempted to ignore it, since tonight's theme was road-trip movies and she hated to break away from *Priscilla, Queen of the Desert* to talk to what was probably a phone salesperson anyway.

But guilt and the worry that it might be a friend in need drove her to hit the pause button and reach over and pluck the phone from its cradle. "Hello?"

"Is this Marlee Jones?"

"That depends on who's calling. Who is this?"

"This is Craig Brinkman."

"Oh, hi, Craig." She smiled and tucked her feet up under her, settling in for a longer conversation. "Nice to talk to you. How are you doing?"

"I'm actually pretty busy right now. I just called to get directions to your place."

"Sure. Or if you want to meet for a drink or something I can bring you a map."

"I don't really have time for that. Just give me your address."

She frowned. Craig wasn't any chattier on the phone than he was via e-mail. "Sure. I'm really easy to find." She rattled off her address and the names of the cross streets.

"Great. I'll pick you up at eight on Saturday morning."

Almost too late, she realized he was about to

hang up. "Wait, wait," she called. "Don't hang up yet."

"What is it?" He came back on the line.

"Is there anything I should bring? Anything you need me to do?"

"No, I already have everything planned out. And I have reservations for hotels along the way."

"You do?" Not that she wasn't aware some people traveled this way; she just never saw the point.

"Yes. That way we don't have to waste any time searching for a place to stay each night."

"What if something happens and we don't make it to the place where you have reservations?"

"What could happen?"

"I don't know—bad weather, construction detours. Or we could get lost." She didn't mention that she *always* got lost at least once on a trip of any length.

"You don't have to worry about that. I have our itinerary all mapped out and I've checked road conditions."

"Oh. Well, I wasn't really worried." She shifted the phone to her other ear. "Are you sure you don't have time for a quick drink? Or a cup of coffee."

"Sorry, but I'm pretty busy here. I'd better go."

Without waiting for her to say good-bye, he hung up. She replaced the phone in its cradle and stared at it, worrying her lower lip between her teeth. Hadn't Mr. Brinkman heard that first impressions counted? He certainly hadn't made a very good one with her.

She sat back on the sofa and stared at the television. The Pause function had timed out and the movie had stopped altogether while she'd been on the phone. Just as well. She couldn't focus on enjoying Guy Pierce in drag until she'd sorted out her reaction to Craig Brinkman.

What she knew about Craig:

A) He didn't waste time on small talk, to the point of brusqueness. Her father would have said he was a "no-nonsense kind of fellow," something Dad approved of. So maybe that wasn't all bad, though it tended to annoy Marlee.

B) He was a planner. Okay, some people were like that. They liked to pretend they were in control. Not her cup of tea but she could live with it.

Besides, she'd taken enough detours in her life to know that you could never, ever, count on things turning out the way you planned them. She'd give Craig's itinerary a day, maybe a day and a half, before something came up to throw it off completely.

C) He wasn't very sociable. Sure, he said he was "busy" but who was so busy he couldn't have a cup of coffee or a single drink? Especially with someone he'd be spending an awful lot of time with in the next week or so. Of course, maybe he reasoned that since he was going to be hanging out with her all week there was no need to worry about getting to know her before then. Men did think like that sometimes.

So this uncomfortable feeling in the pit of her stomach when she thought of Craig didn't mean that he was a bad person. He was different, maybe, than the people she normally chose to hang out with, but that wasn't all bad, was it? It was good to get out and get to know different people. She was all for expanding her horizons.

She sat back and hit the Play button for the movie. Fine. Traveling with Craig Brinkman would be merely another kind of adventure. Maybe not the most fun she'd ever had in a car, but it was better than riding the bus.

Just in case though, it wouldn't hurt to pack the Greyhound schedule.

2

MARLEE was up early Saturday morning, stashing the last few necessities in her suitcase and keeping watch out the front window for her ride. She paced the living-room floor, stopping from time to time to stretch or to fetch some last-minute item to stow in her bags. Anything to burn off the nervous energy humming through her. She couldn't wait to see Susan. And to meet Bryan's friend, Craig.

He was probably a lot nicer guy than he'd sounded on the phone. After all, how much could you really tell from a few minutes' conversation and a single e-mail?

They'd have plenty of time to get to know each other on this trip. She'd probably spend more time with Craig Brinkman in the next week than she had with the last four or five guys she'd dated. Men seemed to prefer her as a friend instead of a girlfriend.

Fine. She'd settle for a friendly relationship with the man who was providing a way for her to get to Susan's wedding. A girl couldn't have too many friends, could she?

A sleek black sedan turned the corner and she pulled back the curtains for a better look. A Beemer. Very up-and-coming professional looking. Not very imaginative, but it definitely looked better than a Greyhound bus, so she wasn't complaining. The car parked at the curb and a tall, dark-haired man unfolded from the front seat. She let out a low whistle. Very, very nice. He wore loose-fitting jeans, a polo shirt that showed off broad shoulders and muscular forearms and dark sunglasses that added a hint of mystery. Why hadn't Susan mentioned her chauffeur was so easy on the eyes?

He slammed the car door shut and headed up the walk toward the main house. Marlee's shoulders slumped. Oh. So maybe this wasn't the right guy after all. She picked up the oversize tote bag she'd stashed next to her suitcase and inventoried the contents once more. Should she take another bottle of water? More sunscreen?

She was in the bathroom searching for another tube of sunscreen when the doorbell rang. She checked the peephole and found Mr. Gorgeous himself on her front porch. She hurried to unfasten the multiple locks and chains. "Hello," she said. "You must be Craig. I'm Marlee."

He nodded. "You didn't tell me you were in the carriage house."

Ouch! Was that any way to start their trip? She purposely flashed her biggest smile. "I didn't? Sorry about that. The main house is 112A. I'm in 112*B*, but quite a few people get the addresses mixed up." *See? It's all your fault you went to the wrong door first.* She held the door wide. "Won't you come in? Can I get you a glass of water or a soda?"

"No thanks." Sunglasses still hiding his eyes, he stepped into the living room and looked around. She wondered what he was thinking. She'd decorated the place herself, in what one friend had dubbed "eclectic kitsch." A row of brightly colored papier-mâché cats from Guatemala lined the mantel over the small gas fireplace, a fuchsia shawl from India was draped over her Salvation Army sofa and a chipped marble garden bench served as her coffee table, while an inflatable palm tree left over from a photo shoot took the place of any living plants.

He frowned at the palm tree. "Are you ready to go?"

"Yes. My luggage is right over here." She started toward the bags she'd stashed to the left of the door.

He shook his head.

She looked at him. "What?"

"I should have known a woman would pack half her closet for just a few days."

The words set her teeth on edge. She faced him, hands on her hips. "We'll be gone over a week. Besides, that's not half my closet. Not even close." One of the best features of the carriage house was a huge walk-in closet. She'd filled the space with clothes to suit her every mood, all bought at bargain prices at the city's best thrift and vintage clothing stores.

He frowned down at her luggage. "Three bags?"

Honestly. Just because a man could get by with one suit, two shirts and pair of jeans didn't mean a woman could! "The big suitcase is clothes and shoes. The small tote is makeup and hair accessories. The larger tote has my laptop, books, snacks and emergency supplies."

"Emergency supplies?"

"Band-Aids, aspirin, sunscreen, stain remover and, uh, other things." She didn't mention the condoms she'd added at the last minute. Not that she was planning anything, but you never knew....

He picked up the suitcase and the larger tote. She locked the door behind her, then followed him to his car. "Thank you for giving me a ride," she said, determined to start off on the right foot with him, despite his less than pleasant demeanor. He was Bryan's friend. She was Susan's friend. There was no reason they shouldn't get along. "Just let me know how much my share of expenses comes to."

"I'll do that." He stashed her totebag in the back seat, then turned and handed her a CD case and a sheaf of computer print-outs. "Your job is to keep the tunes spinning, read this itinerary and schedule I've printed out, and keep quiet."

She stared at him. So much for thinking they could be friends. The guy was a jerk. "You obviously have the wrong impression of me," she said, barely suppressing the urge to rip his head off.

"What do you mean?"

She reached up and removed his sunglasses. He blinked at her. "Hey—"

"I like to look people in the eye when I talk to them," she said. "Let's get this straight. I am not some child or some servant for you to order around or patronize."

Without the sunglasses, he looked less forbidding, though he was still frowning. "I'm going out of my way here to do you a favor."

"And I'm doing you one."

"How's that?"

"I'm keeping you company and paying half the expenses."

"I didn't ask for company."

"No? You agreed to do this, didn't you? You could have said no."

They stared at each other in silence for a long moment. He had eyes the color of toffee, a rich brown with golden flecks. The kind of eyes that could make a woman forget what she'd been arguing about….

He was the first to look away. "You're right. I agreed."

She suppressed a thrill of victory. A man who'd admit he was wrong couldn't be all bad. "So if you have regrets about that, that's your problem, not mine. That doesn't give you the right to make us both miserable."

He winced. "Right again." He took a deep breath and straightened. "I'm sorry I've been such a jerk. Let's start over." He held out his hand. "I'm Craig."

Now this was more like it. The faintest hint of a smile replaced the scowl he'd worn earlier. Much better. The man was definitely easy on the eyes. She slipped her hand into his, warmth traveling through her at his touch like an electric current. "It's nice to meet you, Craig. I'm Marlee."

She didn't know how long they stood there like that, holding hands and staring into each other's eyes. She was dimly aware of traffic moving past, of the distant drone of a lawnmower and a slamming door. These were merely background noise for the fireworks going off in her brain. If she was writing dialogue for the commercial version of the encounter, the only word she would have been able to come up with was *Wow!*

He slipped his hand from hers and took a step back. "Come on," he said. "We've got a long way to go. We'd better get started."

While he guided the car toward the Beltway out of town, she adjusted her seat, then flipped through the CD selection. Lyle Lovett, Shania Twain, Stevie Ray Vaughn. Filed alphabetically. Of course. The man had eclectic tastes. Nothing boring here. She slid the Lyle Lovett disc into the player, and flipped through the sheaf of papers he'd handed her. "What is all this anyway?" she asked.

"The itinerary for our trip. It shows driving directions, mileage between major intersections and the hotels where we'll be staying. I've listed our rest stops, stops for fuel and food, along with local gas prices and information on highway conditions."

She scanned the pages of close print and columns of figures with the horrified fascination of someone perusing an autopsy report. "You must have spent an awful lot of time putting this together," she said.

"It'll save us a lot of time later."

Right. With a week to go until the wedding, they didn't exactly have to race across country to get there in time, but Craig was obviously one of those guys who didn't consider a day on the road worthwhile unless he could set a new record for distance traveled in the shortest time.

She slipped the itinerary under the seat. They could deal with that little problem later.

She studied Craig out of the corner of her eye, trying not to be obvious. He had a good strong jaw and short hair. His hands on the steering wheel looked strong, too, with long fingers and neatly trimmed nails. No ring. Was he divorced? Involved with anyone? Not that she was interested, but she'd been playing the dating game so long such assessments were as automatic as locking her door behind her when she entered her house.

"How do you know Bryan?" she asked.

"We met in college. We were suite mates and both studying business and we really hit it off."

Of course. He was obviously the serious, sensible businessman. Not a flighty artist like her. "What do you do now?"

"I'm a chef." He glanced at her, as if gauging her response to this revelation. "Right now I'm in charge of the Senate Dining Room."

Oh-ho! *Not* a dull businessman. Cooking was creative, wasn't it? She leaned forward, suppressing a buzz of excitement. This trip might prove to be a lot more interesting than she'd anticipated. "I'm impressed. And I have to confess, a little intimidated by a man who can cook better than I can."

His smile was definitely killer. "Not to brag, but I can cook better than most people I know. It comes in handy sometimes."

Now there would be a nice twist—a man who could cook dinner for me, instead of suffering through my own uneven attempts at a meal. And then for dessert... She quickly pulled her mind back from the cliff it was about to dive off. Where had this rampant lust come from? Yeah, it had been a while since she'd had anything like a steady relationship, but since when did handsome strangers inspire such wild fantasies?

Deep breath, she reminded herself, inhaling slowly. Unfortunately, all she could smell was Craig himself, something herbal and spicy and definitely yummy.

She swallowed hard and leaned back in the seat. *Slow down. Make innocuous conversation.* "Do you enjoy your work?" she asked.

"The cooking part, yes. I'm thinking of opening my own restaurant soon."

"You should do it." She tucked one leg under her and arranged her skirt over her lap. *This was more like it. Act casual. Just friends.* "I'm a big believer in doing what makes you happy."

He shook his head. "It's not so easy. Opening your own place involves a lot of risk. Restaurants fail in this town every day."

"Life is risky, though. Isn't it?"

He frowned and she wondered if she'd overdone

the Miss Mary Sunshine routine. People had accused her before of being too much of an optimist.

"What do you do that makes you happy?" he asked after a moment.

"I'm an advertising copywriter for a firm that specializes in non-profits."

"I guess you like the work enough to bring your laptop on vacation with you."

"Oh, I love the work. But the laptop's not for that. It's for my Web diary."

He raised one eyebrow. "Web diary?"

"Yeah, I'm a blogger. I have a Web site where I post writings about what's going on in my life."

"Things like this trip?"

"That's right. I figured I could make notes as ideas strike me during the day, then upload them at the hotel every evening."

"And people read this? Strangers?"

"Yeah, I'm made a lot of cool friends that way. Fans."

He shook his head. "You don't think it's a little odd to have people you don't even know reading about your life?"

She shifted in her seat. "I'm not an idiot. I don't put personal information on there. It just gives me a chance to work on my writing and…I don't know. Make a connection. There are hundreds of bloggers. Thousands. It's another kind of Internet community."

He continued to look skeptical. "Does this diary of yours have a name?"

"It's called *Travels with Marlee.* I write about places I go. Things I see."

"Do you see that many interesting things?"

She nodded. "They're out there, if you keep your eyes open. Every trip is a journey of discovery. That's what the blog is about, really—sharing my discoveries with readers."

"You don't think sometimes you're simply moving from point A to point B in the most efficient manner?"

"This may come as a shock to you, but there are people who think efficiency is overrated."

He glanced at her. "You, for instance?"

"Haven't you heard that getting there is half the fun?"

He shrugged. "And sometimes getting there is merely something you endure to reach your destination."

She leaned toward him. "You wouldn't be talking about this particular trip, would you?"

"Now why would you think that?" The corners of his mouth twitched and she relaxed. He was teasing her. She couldn't help but like a man with a sense of humor, even if he kept it under wraps most of the time.

And she did like Craig, in spite of his scarily organized and exacting ways. She supposed there were advantages to having every journey—and the rest of your life—all laid out neatly. There were probably times when having an idea of what you'd be doing next week or next year was useful.

But what if while making all those plans you missed something even better? It seemed an awfully big risk to her.

"I take it you plan to write about this trip?"

His question interrupted her musings. "Well, yeah. That's what I do."

"Do me a favor and leave me out of it. I don't want strangers reading about me."

"Don't worry. If I mention you at all, I'll give you an assumed name."

"What kind of name?"

"I don't know. I haven't thought of anything yet." She leaned back and dug around in the tote that rested on the floor behind his seat and pulled out two apples. "Want one?"

"Thanks." He accepted the fruit, bit into it, and chewed, looking thoughtful. "I don't think I've ever met anyone like you."

She laughed. "A lot of people say that. This time, I'm going to take it as a compliment."

"Do you look on the bright side of everything?"

"You can either cry or laugh. I prefer to laugh." She leaned back in the seat and took a bite out of her apple. Not that her life was one laugh after the other, but she did try to limit the tears. Anyone who micromanaged things as much as Craig seemed to could use a few more laughs in his life. Maybe she could oblige, and enjoy herself in the process.

But not *too* much. She shifted in her seat as her inner seductress sought once more to make an appearance. What was with her today? She'd have to check the ingredients on the power bar she'd had for breakfast. Maybe it contained some secret aphrodisiac.

She glanced at the man in the driver's seat. He was intent on traffic, apparently oblivious to the effect he was having on her and her libido. That figured. She was lusting after Handsome here and he was figuring out the best route through Virginia. That was the story of her life, wasn't it? They might be in the same car, but once again, she was headed in the wrong direction.

HERE *I am on the road again, this time headed to California. My chauffeur is a man who wishes to remain anonymous, so I'll be referring to him as "the Chef." This trip is definitely shaping up unlike any other*

I've taken. Not to say the Chef is uptight or anything, but the man has a schedule planned down to the minute. When we stop for gas, he figures his mileage and records it in a little notebook he keeps in his glove compartment, along with the date and the price of the gas. When I suggested we make a little detour through Winchester, Virginia, to see the World's Largest Apple (Red Delicious, natch!) he looked at me like I was a nut. I can see I'm going to have to educate him on the Travels with Marlee *philosophy—never pass up a chance for adventure!*

Hasn't he heard the point of a vacation is to relax? Still, he's a nice guy when he loosens up, and I appreciate him giving me a lift to Susan's wedding. And who knows? I've got the next few days to convince him to slow down and make room in his life for adventure. After all, this wouldn't be Travels with Marlee *without a few detours along the way, would it?*

MARLEE fell asleep shortly after they crossed into Virginia, her legs drawn up beside her, her head resting against the window. Craig glanced at her every few minutes, enjoying the view. She wasn't what you'd call a stunning woman, but she had an intriguing, gamin quality—short brown hair and huge dark eyes set against pale skin. And that damned wide-eyed optimism of hers was coupled with an oversize self-confidence.

When she'd called him on the carpet this morning over his jerky behavior, he'd been struck dumb with awe. He couldn't help but admire anyone who seemed so sure of herself.

He still wasn't sure about spending the week traveling with her, though. The whole reason he was driving to California instead of flying was to have the time alone. He'd purposely set aside two weeks for the trip out and back and planned his route to give him plenty of time to get to the wedding and relax beforehand. He had some important decisions to make about his future and this would be a good time to sort things out in his head. The last thing he needed was a woman along. She'd throw off his schedule completely and he wouldn't get a moment's peace.

Quit your whining, Brinkman. You said you'd do this, so time to gut it up and do it. He had to admit he'd enjoyed Marlee's company so far. He smiled, remembering all her talk about the importance of doing work you loved. That was certainly a different way to look at things. He wondered what his dad would say if Craig tried out that argument. Dad had wanted him to be a banker or an architect. To his way of thinking, cooking was something women did. He was still waiting for Craig to "come to his senses" and get a real job.

If only he could make Dad see that being a chef *was* a real job, and he had the potential to be a big success at it. It was all part of his five-year plan: establish a customer base and get on-the-job training working for someone else, then open his own place inside the Loop. He'd already completed the first part of his plan. After three years at the Senate Dining Room, he felt ready to strike out on his own. But it was still risky. He had to find the right location, design the perfect menu and make sure he had enough financial backing. He wanted to be certain of every detail before he made his move.

Marlee sighed and shifted in her seat, smiling to herself. What was she so happy about? And why did was he suddenly happier, just being in the same car

with her? Obviously he'd been neglecting his social
life too much if simply being with a woman he hardly
knew could make him this lightheaded.

Not that he didn't date when he had the chance,
but he wasn't in any rush to get involved in a long-
term relationship. He certainly wasn't rushing to the
altar like Bryan.

He still couldn't believe his best friend—his last
single buddy—was tying the knot. What was the rush
to get married all of a sudden? Bryan was the same
age he was, twenty-eight. They had plenty of time.

The way Craig figured it, he'd get himself established in his career before he took on the added responsibility of marriage and raising a family. Say,
around age thirty-five sounded right. Then he'd find
a woman who was successful in her own right, someone capable and dependable like himself.

Eyes still closed, as if struggling to hold on to
sleep a little longer, Marlee unfolded her legs and
stretched her arms overhead. Her slow, sensuous
movements made him think of lazy mornings spent
in bed and languid lovemaking in tangled sheets,
things he seldom indulged in. She arched her back
against the seat and her breasts jutted against the
thin fabric of her dress, and he felt an immediate
physical response.

He forced his eyes away. He wasn't going to get
involved with this chick. She was sweet, but she definitely wasn't his type—and the last thing he needed
in his life right now was any more complications. He
had too much else to think about. He'd get his career
on the right track, and then he could work on the relationship side of things.

"Where are we?" she asked, her voice soft with
sleep.

"Somewhere outside of Roanoke, Virginia. I'm hoping to make Kingsport, Tennessee by dark, but the traffic around Fairfax put us behind." Too far behind for his liking. They'd have to make up some time to get back on schedule.

"What time is it?" She leaned toward the dashboard clock, squinting in the glare.

"Lunch time. I've been looking for a place to stop, but there isn't any." And they weren't anywhere near his planned stop. The last town they'd passed had been little more than a post office and a service station. Since then, the view had been mostly trees and fields.

"That's okay. We can have a picnic." She reached back into her bag and began taking out items and piling them in her lap. "I've got some cheese. Crackers. Summer sausage. Grapes. A chocolate bar."

He suppressed a laugh. Any minute now he expected her to pull out half a roast chicken and a bottle of wine. She turned to him once more. "It's enough to tide us over until we can have a real meal."

"Sounds great. I'll look for a place to pull over."

A few miles farther on, they spotted a sign for a roadside park. "Pull in there," she directed.

He parked under a shady oak and they carried the food and two bottles of water to a picnic table. The air smelled of freshly mown grass and the wild irises that bloomed on the bank of a stream running through the little park.

While she arranged the meal on the table, he walked over to the stream and stooped to rinse his face and hands. He spotted bunches of watercress growing at the water's edge and picked some.

"What's this?" she asked when he offered her the greens.

"Watercress." He tore off some of the crisp herb and popped it in his mouth. "The same stuff they use to make fancy tea sandwiches."

She grinned and helped herself to the greens. "I guess if we run out of food, you'll be able to forage for us. Do they teach that kind of thing in chef's school?"

"The Culinary Institute didn't take field trips to pick wild greens, no." He took a seat on top of the picnic table, his feet on the bench below. "I learned about this stuff on my grandparents' farm."

"And where was that?" She sliced off a thick round of summer sausage and offered it to him.

"Arkansas. I spent every summer there." He grinned. "I couldn't wait for school to be out so I could go."

"Where was home the rest of the time?" She topped a cracker with cheese and popped the whole thing into her mouth.

"New Mexico. A little town not too far from Farmington."

"Is your family still there?"

He nodded. "My mom and dad and two sisters." He grinned. "I'm the black sheep, moved all the way out to D.C." His tone was light, but the words weren't too far from truth. He'd always been the different one in his family, the one who was never satisfied.

"That's practically on the way to San Diego, isn't it?" she asked. "We should stop and say hello."

He shook his head. The last thing he wanted right now was to see his dad and have to listen to another lecture on getting his act together. If he told his father he was thinking of opening his own restaurant, the old man would have a stroke. No matter that Craig knew exactly what he had to do to make this work. "We don't have time for that."

"Sure we do. The wedding's almost ten days away."

He helped himself to more sausage. "Where is your family from?" he asked, anxious to change the subject.

"Dimmitt, Texas. Can you believe it? They're all horrified that I've gone off to the big city to consort with politicians and lobbyists and other evil-doers." Her eyes widened in mock horror and he laughed again. In fact, he'd laughed more in the past three hours than he had in the past three months.

"You have a nice smile," she said, helping herself to a grape. "Much better than that scowl you showed up with this morning."

"Yeah, well..." He looked away. "I guess I wasn't looking forward to this trip much."

"Because of me...or for some other reason?"

"For a lot of reasons, I guess." He rolled his shoulders. "Bryan's my last single buddy. Makes me feel...I don't know. Out of step."

"Yeah." The wistfulness in her voice surprised him. He looked at her again. She rolled a grape back and forth between her palms, seemingly unaware of the movement. As if she felt him watching her, she looked up. "Are you seeing anyone? I mean, anyone special?"

Something in her voice sent a prickle of awareness down his spine. "No, you?" He held his breath, waiting for her answer.

She shook her head. "Nope."

The atmosphere was charged like the air under a high-voltage line. Suddenly they weren't only two people on a trip together, but a man and a woman. Both unattached. The word itself implied something unfinished. Two halves looking to be made whole.

Now where had *that* thought come from? He

launched himself off the table, eager to put some distance between himself and these disturbing feelings. But she was right behind him, running past him to the creek, where she kicked off her shoes and began wading in the shallows.

He followed, the cool water lapping at his ankles, gravel massaging his toes. Holding her arms out like a tightrope walker, she picked her way across a half-submerged log toward the middle of the stream. "Careful," he called.

She looked back over her shoulder, eyes bright, teasing. "Come on," she called. "It's fun."

He shook his head. The log was green with moss. Probably slippery as hell.

She walked out farther, and struck a ballerina's pose, balanced on one leg. His heart pounded as she teetered back and forth. He checked the water—it looked deep under where she stood. Did she know how to swim? Would he have time to save her in the swift current? "Come back before you fall," he said, his voice gruff.

She laughed, a musical sound in harmony with the cadence of the tumbling water. Sunlight spotlighted her hair and touched her skin with gold. "Come and get me!" she called.

He told himself he wouldn't let her bait him. He would turn around and go back to the car and wait for her to follow. They didn't have time for silly games like this.

But the next thing he knew, he was taking one tentative step out onto the log, and then another. The moss was cool and slick beneath his feet, but he could feel the rougher bark beneath it. He kept his eyes on her, telling himself not to look down. She beckoned, like some wild water sprite. "We'd better go," he said, even as he continued feeling his way toward her. "We have a lot of miles to cover."

"We needed a break." She turned her back on him and walked even farther out on the log.

He decided he really would turn around now. What did he think he was going to do when he reached her anyway? He'd already decided giving in to the desire she stirred in him was a bad idea.

He started to pivot to face the other direction, but as he did so, he felt the log shudder, and out of the corner of his eye, he caught a glimpse of windmilling arms.

In an instant, he lunged forward and caught her, steadying her against him even as he fought to stay upright himself. Heart pounding, breath coming in gasps, he clung to her until they were both still. The only sounds were the rasp of his own breathing and the gurgle of the creek as it slid beneath their makeshift bridge.

She smiled up at him, eyes wide, lips slightly parted. "Thanks," she said. "I guess my sense of balance isn't much better than my sense of direction."

"You're crazy, you know that?" he asked.

She nodded. "You say that like it's a bad thing."

She had movie-star eyes, dark and impossibly luminous. Looking into them, he forgot all about the miles they had to cover or the disaster they'd narrowly avoided. All his senses were focused on the feel of her in his arms. She was the stuff of bedroom fantasies and early-morning dreams.

"Are you going to stand there staring, or are you going to kiss me?"

Her voice was breathy, as beckoning as her gestures had been moments before.

His lips were on hers before she'd finished speaking. She tasted like fresh fruit and peppery watercress. She rose on tiptoe, angling her lips more fully against his, opening to him, her tongue teasing across his teeth. He slipped both hands behind her neck, his fingers sliding up into her hair as he deepened the kiss, losing himself in the sheer pleasure of the moment.

The sound of a car door slamming shattered the spell she'd cast over him. He flinched, and braced one foot behind him on the log to keep from falling. Marlee opened her eyes and blinked. Voices were approaching. "Looks like we have company," he said.

She nodded, and slipped out of his arms, avoiding his gaze. A blush stained her cheeks the color of ripe strawberries. Still clutching her hand, he led the way off the log, but she broke away from him as soon as they were on land again, and headed for the picnic table, where she began gathering the remains of their lunch.

He stopped to collect their shoes from the bank, then followed more slowly, letting himself cool down a little. What exactly had happened back there, other than the closest thing he'd ever known to spontaneous combustion?

3

WITH SHAKING HANDS, Marlee gathered up the leftovers from their lunch and stashed them in her bag. What had she been thinking, practically jumping Craig's bones there on that log? Sure, he was a hottie and yummy as a hot fudge sundae, but what kind of a woman throws herself at a man she's known all of three hours? He'd think she was desperate, or cheap—or both.

She headed for the car and he came up behind her as she was arranging things in the back seat. "About what happened just now..." he began.

She whirled to face him, her face hot with embarrassment. "It didn't mean anything," she blurted. "I mean...it just happened. And it shouldn't have." She stared at the ground. This was coming out badly.

"Yeah, uh, I guess we both got a little carried away."

She risked a glance at him and saw that he had his head down, his hands shoved in his pockets. She relaxed a little. He didn't look like a guy who'd gotten the wrong idea. He dug a trench in the gravel with the toe of his shoe. "Look, not that it's an excuse or anything, but it's been a while for me and..." He shook his head. "I don't want you to think that because I'm giving you a ride, I think you owe me anything. Because I don't. Think that. I mean, I'm not like that."

Something in her melted right then. It was all she

could do not to throw her arms around him again. For a guy who had come on this morning like Mr. Macho, she liked this version even better. Call him Mr. Decent. How many of those did you meet anymore? "It's okay," she said. "I guess…." She shrugged. "I guess we could say we both did what came naturally. But that doesn't mean it meant anything." Except she'd been on plenty of nature walks, camping trips and day hikes before and fresh air had never affected her this way.

"Right." He nodded and took his hands out of his pockets. Their eyes met, then they both looked away, as if afraid to focus too closely on each other just yet. "So, we both agree we'll go on like before. As if nothing happened."

"Right." Should she warn him that at various times she'd also sworn off chocolate, coffee and ice cream, and hadn't managed to stay away from any of those temptations longer than a week? But then, a week was all she needed, right?

"So, I guess we'd better hit the road if we're going to make it to Kingsport by dark."

He started around the car to the driver's side, but she stopped him. "Let me drive for a while. You can take a nap."

He shook his head. "That's okay."

"Oh, come on. We'll make better time and be more alert if we take turns driving." Besides, this was another way to keep things even between them. Not that she didn't believe what he'd said about her not owing him any "special" favors for agreeing to give her a lift, but she didn't want any room for doubt.

He frowned. "I thought you didn't have a license."

A picky detail. "Yes, but that was just bad luck. I'm not a bad driver, really."

He shook his head. "Thanks for the offer, but I'll pass."

"Come on. We're out in the middle of nowhere." She spread her arms wide. "It's a nice, straight road. What could happen?"

He stifled a yawn.

"See, you *are* tired!" She took a step toward him.

He started to back up and bumped into the car. "I'm the only one who's ever driven this car and I think it should stay that way." He put his hand on the side panel, a protective gesture.

"I get it now. You're worried I'll hurt your precious car."

He looked uncomfortable, but she saw she'd scored a bull's-eye. What was it with men and their cars, anyway? "Look, if you're tired, don't you think the chances are greater that you'll have an accident? Whereas I've already had a nap and I'm fresh and alert." She leaned closer, almost but not quite touching him. "I promise I won't let anything happen to your precious car."

Confronted by her in such close quarters, he apparently decided to relent. "Okay, okay. You can drive. But only for a little while." He held out the keys. "And no speeding. Be careful."

She traced an X over her heart. "I promise. I'll take it nice and easy. And you can get some rest."

They got in the car and he pushed the seat back and reclined it slightly. She slipped on her sandals then started the engine. "See, this was a good idea," she said.

He nodded. "Maybe you're right. I mean, how much trouble could anybody get into way out here?"

MARLEE GRIPPED the steering wheel so tightly her fingers were practically fused to the leather. She gnawed her lower lip and tried to think calming thoughts. *Deep breaths*, she reminded herself. *Take deep breaths. There's no need to panic.*

Except that she didn't have a clue where she was, or even if she was headed in the right direction. She glanced over at Craig. Head back, mouth open, he snored softly. Thank God he wasn't awake to see her predicament. Though if he was, he might be able to get them out of this mess.

She'd done fine for the first hour or so, cruising along at a nice safe speed, humming in harmony with Bonnie Rait on the stereo, enjoying the beautiful spring day.

Then one of those nasty orange signs had popped up on the side of the road. One that said Road Construction Ahead. And then an even nastier sign had appeared. Detour.

She'd sat up a little straighter in the seat and told herself she could handle it. All she had to do was follow the signs and she'd end up back on the highway, traveling in the same direction. No problem.

Except she must have missed one of the signs, or maybe they'd forgotten to put one out. She made two or three turns and by that time she was so confused, she couldn't have said *which* way was the right way to go.

So she guessed. A dangerous proposition, but the only other alternative was to wake Craig and ask for help. What self-respecting woman wanted to do that? Especially one who had made such a big deal about driving?

She shifted in the seat, trying to get more comfortable, and stared down the road, hoping for a road sign or a billboard or anything to tell her where she was and where she needed to go. But all she saw were empty fields and distant trees. No houses, no people and no signs.

Keep driving, she told herself. *You're bound to come to a town eventually. That's what roads do. They connect towns.*

She glanced at Craig again. His hair was ruffled and dark beard stubble showed along his jaw. She imagined he'd look like this first thing in the morning.

Her imagination quickly stripped him of his shirt, and painted a picture of him reaching for her across the rumpled sheets....

Stop that! She jerked her gaze back to the road, and tried to ignore the very different kind of heat scorching through her body. This was insane. She didn't usually behave this way with the men she dated. And she had to travel three thousand miles with Craig. She couldn't keep looking at him like a dieter contemplating the dessert of the day. She was an adult. She ought to be able to control these...these urges, and relate to Craig like another adult. A friend. A very sexy, very male friend.

She stifled a groan and clutched the steering wheel even more tightly. Why couldn't they have met back in Washington? Gotten to know each other over a few weeks? Then they could fall into bed guilt-free. But not on a cross-country trip when they were still practically strangers.

What did it matter? He obviously wasn't interested. Oh, his body was, but you couldn't trust a man's physical reactions. They could get turned on by pictures in magazines or random hints of certain perfumes. So when she'd come on to Craig back there by the creek, she would have been amazed if he *hadn't* responded.

His mind wasn't interested, though. He'd made that clear up front. He didn't want any "complications." Which she figured was a polite way of saying he didn't want her. Mr. Strictly Business wasn't interested in Ms. Anything Goes. What else was new?

She passed a house, and then another. A small billboard urged her to shop at Dave's Auto Parts in Downieville. Half a mile farther a green sign announced that she was entering Downieville, population thirteen hundred. And three. Relief flooded her. She'd stop at a gas station or grocery store in Downieville and ask for directions. She checked Craig. He still slept soundly. With any luck, she could find out what she needed to know and head back in the right direction before he ever realized what was going on.

As she guided the car down the two-lane through the center of town, nostalgia overwhelmed her. Downieville reminded her of Dimmitt, with its mom-and-pop stores, signs in the windows celebrating the accomplishments of the local school teams and flower boxes along the sidewalks. It looked like the kind of place that would be fun to poke around in, if they had more time.

The town was small, but busy for a Saturday afternoon. People filled the sidewalks in front of the neat rows of shops, and traffic was heavy. Cars, trucks, even a fire engine clogged the street up ahead. Had there been an accident? Or maybe there was a big game.

She followed the stream of cars, inching past sidewalks lined with people. Some had even brought lawn chairs and sat down to watch. Some of them waved to her, and she waved back. She rolled down a window, intending to ask a passerby what was going on. Just then, a band started up, trumpets and a big bass drum loud in her ears.

She looked behind her and indeed, a high-school

band, complete with a trio of twirlers in leotards, marched in formation behind her car. Beyond them, she could see a truck pulling a trailer decorated with crêpe-paper flowers. Facing forward again, she saw two clowns skipping ahead of her, bunches of balloons in their hands.

The band let out another loud fanfare. "Huh? Wha—?" Craig sat up, rubbing his eyes. He looked around, blinking. "Where are we? What's going on?"

She watched one of the clowns hand a balloon to a giggling toddler. "I think we're in a parade." Ahead of them in the traffic, she could make out a red convertible, with a tiara-clad young woman perched on the back seat. She tossed out candy, and the children scrambled for it.

"A parade! Are you crazy?"

"Look in my tote and get that bag of hard candy, will you?"

"What?"

"Just do it." She smiled and gave her best Miss America wave to the passing crowd.

Craig handed her the candy. "How did we end up in a parade?"

Ignoring him, she ripped open the bag and tossed a handful of candy out the window. It landed short of the sidewalk and children rushed to gather it up. "Smile," she told him. "Everyone's watching."

He looked around, scowl still firmly in place. "I can't believe this."

"Here. Throw some on your side." She shoved candy into his hand. "It's fun."

Looking doubtful, he rolled down the window on his side and threw out a handful of candy. One of the clowns strolled over and handed him a balloon. "What am I supposed to do with this?" he asked, but the clown had already moved on to the car ahead of them.

"How sweet!" Marlee laughed at a boy and his dog who watched the parade from the back of a pickup parked at the curb. "Do you need more candy?"

"What I need is to know how we got into this mess," he said.

"Maybe I thought it would be fun to visit the strawberry festival." She pointed to the banner stretched across the street in front of them. Downieville Strawberry Festival! it proclaimed.

"Downieville's not on our route. And we don't have time for this. We're already behind schedule."

"Oh, stuff your schedule!" She spoke without rancor, still smiling and waving to the crowd. All the cars and trucks and floats turned in beneath the sign, which appeared to be the entrance to the local high school.

As Marlee pulled into a parking space and shut off the engine, a round, crinkly-faced man with straw-blond hair and bright blue eyes rushed up to them. "Welcome to Downieville," he said, thrusting his hand in the open driver's-side window. "I'm Ed Hoskins, the mayor. I saw you folks get caught up in our parade. Thanks for getting into the spirit of things."

"Pleased to meet you, Mayor Hoskins. I'm Marlee and this is Craig. You have a wonderful little town."

"Glad to meet you. And thank you." He shook both their hands, though Craig continued to frown. "We think Downieville's a special place. Now y'all come inside and join in the festivities. We've got all kinds of craft and food booths. Games. Fun for everyone." He opened the door and ushered Marlee out.

Craig joined them. "Sir, I —" he began.

"Ed, we've got a problem!" A harried-looking older woman rushed up to them. She gave Marlee and Craig a brief smile. "Sorry to interrupt, but I need the mayor's help here."

"Nancy, what is it?" the mayor asked.

"Doc Nelson had to leave to deliver Sue Nicholson's baby, and he was supposed to judge the bake-off. Now we're a judge short."

"I'm sure we can find someone who won't mind tasting all those delicious pies and cakes for a good cause." The mayor turned back to Marlee and Craig. "You'll want to stick around for this, folks. After the judging, the goodies are sold by the slice. The money goes to our summer youth program."

"Craig can be your judge," Marlee said. "He's a famous Washington, D.C., chef."

"I don't think I—"

Craig started to back away, but she caught hold of his arm. "You'd be perfect," she said. "And we'd be helping these nice people out of a jam."

"A jam! Strawberry jam! We have that, too." The mayor put his arm around Craig's shoulder and led them toward the high-school gym. "A famous chef. Imagine that! Wait until I tell the committee."

Craig looked back over his shoulder and glared at Marlee. She pretended not to notice. So what if this wasn't exactly part of their planned itinerary? Craig worried too much about things like schedules and plans. He needed to learn to relax more. To slow down and smell the roses. Or the strawberries.

CRAIG SPENT the next hour sampling strawberry pies, strawberry cakes, strawberry cookies and muffins. Women and men of all shapes and sizes presented their creations with attitudes ranging from great solemnity to open flirtation. "I know you're going to love this," cooed one buxom blonde. "It's my specialty."

"Stop wasting the man's time, Victoria." An older woman with a face like a bulldog shoved the blonde out of the way and fixed Craig with a stern stare. "Young man, if you're really a famous chef, then you'll recognize my award-winning strawberry pie as the best in the state. I developed the recipe myself and it's never failed to win a ribbon." The words held a definite threat.

Craig managed to keep a smile on his face as he picked up his fork. "I'm sure it's delicious." He gave an equally friendly smile to the blonde. "As I'm sure yours is, too." Who knew judging a small-town baking contest would be so rife with intrigue and danger?

When the women moved on, shooed away by one of the bake-off organizers, Craig looked around the crowded gym for Marlee. He spotted her over by a face-painting booth. Dressed in an oversize red apron, she was painting a butterfly on a little girl's cheek. Marlee had a strawberry painted on her own face. Her hair was tousled and she looked like a kid herself, and every bit as happy.

He didn't buy her story about wanting to stop off at the Strawberry Festival. She must have gotten lost because there was no Downieville listed on his route plan for their trip. Amazing. How could a person get lost on a straight highway?

"Mr. Brinkman? It's time to announce our winners." Nancy, the gray-haired women in charge of the bake-off, led him to the small stage at one end of the gym. While she alerted the crowd that it was time to discover the winners of the contest, he shuffled through the notes he'd made on index cards. One advantage of being a stranger here was that he had no idea who had baked the winning entry, so he could be sure he'd judged fairly. He only hoped the losers wouldn't come after him with a lynch rope.

He looked out at the crowd gathering around him and felt transported back to the junior-high talent show he'd entered when he was thirteen. He'd spent weeks rehearsing his act, but when he'd taken the stage in a gymnasium very much like this one, he'd been paralyzed with fear and had made a mess of things. When he'd heard everyone laughing, he'd run off the stage and vowed never to put himself in that position again.

"And now, our special celebrity judge, Chef Craig Brinkman, from Washington, D.C., will announce our winners."

The sound of his name brought him out of his trance. He stepped forward, clutching his stack of index cards, and cleared his throat. "The first runner-up is the strawberry pound cake, um, number seventeen."

Squeals erupted to the left of the platform and a teenage girl rushed forward, pausing every few feet to embrace an enthusiastic friend. She accepted her purple ribbon from Craig, then turned to beam at the crowd while a woman who must have been her mother snapped half a dozen photos. For all her excitement, you'd have thought the girl had won the Pillsbury bake-off. Here in Downieville, the Strawberry Festival was apparently just as big.

He waited for the commotion to die down, then consulted his next card. "Third place goes to the chocolate strawberry cake. Number twenty-seven."

Laughter greeted this announcement. After a pause, a burly young man wearing a letter jacket from the local high school shuffled to the platform. The group of high-school girls giggled and whispered behind their hands as he approached. Apparently things hadn't changed all that much since Craig's school days. A boy who cooked was still something of a novelty.

"What's your name, son?" he asked as he shook the young man's hand.

"Uh, it's Mike. Mike Brewster."

"Congratulations, Mike. You might make a great chef someday."

Mike looked uncertain, then grinned. "Thanks. I guess that's pretty cool, huh?"

"I always thought so."

As Mike returned to his place at the back of the crowd, he walked with an extra swagger, his shoulders straight. "Did you hear what he said?" He showed the ribbon to his friends. "He said I could be a great chef—like him."

"Second place goes to the strawberry tart. Number forty-eight."

The sour-faced woman who'd confronted him earlier made her way to the platform with much dignity. She accepted the second-place ribbon without a smile. "I'll have you know this is the first time my strawberry tart has failed to take first place," she said. "That's what happens when you bring in outside judges. All that fancy *nouveau cuisine* has obviously ruined your tastebuds for good, American cooking."

He tried not to cringe, and reminded himself that he would in all likelihood never have to see this woman again. Thank God for that.

"And now, the moment you've all been waiting for." Now that he'd been up here a while, he wasn't so nervous. "I have to say, this was a really tough choice. Most of the entries were excellent and you are all to be commended."

"Just tell us who won!" a man shouted from the back.

"Right." He double-checked his notes. "The winner is the strawberry cream tart, number forty-seven."

A woman squealed and the next thing he knew the buxom blonde was on stage beside him, her arms wrapped around him. "I told you you'd love it," she exclaimed, and kissed him soundly, to the laughter and hooting of the crowd.

Somehow he managed to extricate himself from her grip while Nancy distracted her with the trophy. He took out his handkerchief to wipe lipstick off his face. As kisses went, this had been nothing spectacular.

Now his kiss by the creek with Marlee—*that* had been a spectacular kiss. A woman who could kiss like that didn't need to know how to cook. It made him wonder what other "special talents" she might possess.

Don't go there, he told himself. That kiss had been a mistake. He couldn't imagine what had come over him. Maybe the watercress he'd picked was some wild hybrid, with hallucinogenic properties. How else to explain his sudden attraction to a woman who was so far from his ideal match it was ludicrous? No sense wasting their time with each other. The thing to do was to get back on the road and get to the wedding as quickly as possible.

4

MARLEE WATCHED the announcement of the bake-off winners from the face-painting booth, where she'd been recruited to put her artistic skills to use. At first, Craig looked pretty nervous up there on the stage, but after a while he relaxed more. And the crowd loved him. More than one woman had commented on how handsome he was, and how exciting it was to have a "celebrity" in their midst.

She'd allowed herself to feel a little smug. Not that she had any claim on Craig or anything, but they were traveling together, so people *thought* there was something between them. What woman wouldn't like people thinking she had what it took to attract a great-looking, "famous" guy? They didn't have to know the only hold she had on Craig was a mutual friendship with Susan and Bryan, and the memory of their scorching roadside kiss.

A kiss she hadn't been able to put out of her mind since. The move had been completely out of character for her, but the more she thought about it, the more she realized it was entirely appropriate for her current situation. After all, hadn't she said she was going to use this trip to cut loose a little? To explore other options?

Fate had brought her together with a sexy man who was definitely different from the men she usually favored, so why not make the most of it? Here was her chance to have a no-guilt fling. After this trip, she'd probably never see Craig again. No one she worked with and none of her friends would ever even know this had happened.

She smiled at the thought. The only trick would be convincing Craig to go along with the idea, but if the kiss they'd shared had been any indicator, that might not be so tough to do.

The smile faded as she watched him congratulate the first place winner with a no-holds-barred lip-lock. She stared, open-mouthed, as the blonde wrapped her arms around him. People were starting to comment when the two finally came up for air.

Marlee looked away, her pulse pounding at her temples with the beginning of a headache. So maybe she'd misjudged again. Obviously, Craig kissed women at the drop of the hat. What had been a memorable moment for her had been routine for him.

She faked a smile for the little boy who'd approached the booth, ticket in hand. "Hi there, honey," she said. "What would you like painted on your face?"

She was putting the finishing touches on a spider on the little boy's face when Craig approached. "We need to be going," he said.

"There you go, Tyler. Go scare some girls." She patted the boy's shoulder and sent him off to terrorize a group of giggling girls who stood nearby. Then she started cleaning her paintbrush.

"Did you hear me?" Craig said. "We need to get going."

"What's your rush?" she said, not looking at him. "Don't you want to stay and talk to your fans? Maybe pass out a few more kisses."

"What the—" He leaned closer, his voice strained.

"If you're talking about what happened up there on the stage, *she* kissed *me*. She was excited about winning." He stepped back. "Not that it's any of your business."

"Of course it's not." She dropped the clean brushes in a glass of fresh water. Her instinct was to read him the riot act but that wasn't possible with so many people around. That was one bad thing about small towns—if she and Craig argued, it would be all over town by nightfall.

"We need to get back on the road," he said again.

"Oh, you really should stay for the dance tonight." A woman with bright-red hair came around from the other side of the booth.

"Craig, this is Clara, Mayor Hoskins's wife," Marlee introduced them.

"Roger and the Renegades are playing," Clara explained. "They're very good."

Craig's smile was weak. "We really need to get on the road if we're going to find a room for the night."

"Abingdon is an hour away, and you'll never find a room there anyway, what with the regional basketball championship tournament there this weekend." Clara patted his arm. "I already told your wife you could stay with us. We have a spare bedroom. It's not fancy, but it's comfortable."

She bustled away to greet a new customer, leaving them alone. Craig pulled Marlee aside. "She thinks we're married?"

Marlee flushed. "I sort of let her think that."

"Why?"

She shrugged out of his grasp. "This is a small town. I didn't want them to think we were, you know. Fooling around."

"We're *not* fooling around!"

Only because *he'd* rather kiss total strangers. Or maybe he *preferred* big-breasted blondes.

Who was she kidding? Every man preferred big-breasted blondes. Why else was Pamela Anderson a millionaire?

The lines fanning out from the corners of his eyes deepened and he lowered his voice. "You couldn't simply tell them we're only traveling together?"

"This isn't the kind of place where people do that." She looked into his eyes, silently pleading for him to go along with this ridiculous charade. "I know. I grew up in a town like this."

He shook his head. "This is the twenty-first century."

"Yes, but people in small towns aren't as…progressive. It's sweet, really." And annoying sometimes, too. But they weren't staying long enough for it to truly get on her nerves, as it probably would within a few days.

He let out a deep breath. "So what are we going to do?"

"Why don't we spend the night here and get a fresh start in the morning?"

"Do you even know how to get back to the interstate from here?"

She hung her head and mumbled something about asking directions. She'd really hoped they could avoid this discussion.

"You got lost, didn't you?"

"There was a detour. And they must not have had all the signs out." She set her mouth in a stubborn pout. "Anyone would have gotten mixed up."

"Uh-huh. How long did you keep driving after you realized you were lost?"

She looked away again, not answering.

He put one finger under her chin and tilted her head up until he was looking into her eyes again. He had such beautiful eyes. Distracting eyes. Dangerous eyes. "How long?" he asked.

"An hour?"

"An hour? Why didn't you stop and ask directions? Or look at the map?"

She began to laugh. She couldn't help it. He was acting as if this was a major disaster, on a par with wrecking the car or losing all their cash. "Where's your sense of adventure? Sometimes the best things happen when you just go along for the ride and wait to see what happens next."

"I think that's what I'm afraid of." He turned and stalked away, leaving her to wait on her next customer.

She smiled and hummed to herself as she mixed paint on her pallet. Craig was grumpy now, but he'd come around. In any case, he'd stopped insisting they leave Downieville right this minute.

Score one for the female half of their dynamic duo. Craig didn't know it yet, but he was on his way to coming around to her way of thinking, she was sure of it. It was only a matter of time.

DOWNIEVILLE, Virginia, Strawberry Festival. An unexpected detour (well, is there any other kind when I'm along for the ride?) took us to this post-card-perfect small town in the Appalachian foothills. We threw ourselves into the festivities right off the bat by riding in the parade, then the Chef was asked to judge the strawberry bake-off. I helped out at the face-painting booth. (I may have discovered a hidden talent.) After a supper of country-fried chicken and divine strawberry shortcake, I think even the Chef is starting to mellow. I'll write more later; now it's off to the Strawberry Street Dance!

ROGER AND the Renegades turned out to be a halfway decent band. They played a lively mixture of rock classics with the occasional romantic standard. Marlee stood on the edge of the gym and watched couples jitterbugging around the room. Craig fidgeted beside her. She knew he was still upset about this deviation from his planned route. People like him needed to accept that life seldom went according to plan. You had to be ready for surprises along the way.

He'd changed into a starched dress shirt and gray slacks for the evening, while she'd opted for a lemon-yellow gauze sundress from India. She looked as if she was on her way to a fun party, while he looked as though he was on his way to court.

Not that the outfit didn't suit him. The crisp tailored cotton of his shirt stretched across his shoulders and drew attention to his narrow waist. The slacks fit perfectly as well, and shouted "expensive, good taste." Whereas her dress had come from Indira's Indian Fashion Hut and it probably showed.

The band swung into a new number and she grabbed his hand. "Let's dance."

He hung back. "No, thanks."

"Come on. We're stuck here for the evening. Let's have some fun."

Maybe because he didn't want to make a scene he let her lead him onto the dance floor. She did a few twirls around him, smiling encouragingly. A man this good-looking had to know how to dance, didn't he?

He could dance. Once he'd loosened up, he was quite a good dancer. Not one for fancy moves, but competent. "See, I told you this was fun," she called over the music.

He pulled her close to him. "I've spent worse evenings." But his eyes glinted with humor.

She twirled away and moved around to his other side. "Did you know this is the sixty-seventh Strawberry Festival in Downieville?" she asked.

"I believe the mayor mentioned it five or six times." He grinned. "You don't know how hard it was for me to keep a straight face every time he referred to you as my 'wife.'"

"Shhh." She looked around them, but no one was paying attention. "It won't hurt you to pretend."

"No, but you have to admit, we're an unlikely pair."

She frowned. What did he mean by that remark? "We're about the same age. We're both from D.C. Why wouldn't they think we belong together?"

He clasped both her hands and they spun together. "A stranger might make that mistake, but anyone who knew us would laugh. I mean, we're complete opposites."

The comment annoyed her. Did he think a woman like her wasn't good enough for someone like him? "Haven't you heard opposites attract?"

"That only works in movies and books."

"I don't know. I thought we attracted pretty well back there at the creek." She shimmied closer to him. Had he forgotten that kiss so soon? (At least he'd stayed away from the blonde and the half-dozen other women who'd insisted on stopping by to flirt with him. Whether it was because she'd warned him off or because he truly wasn't interested didn't matter to her at this point.)

The smoldering look he gave her told her he hadn't forgotten at all. "Physical attraction is different from true compatibility."

"I don't know. I think it's an awfully good place

to start." Just then the music stopped, and she and Craig were left standing face to face in the relative quiet, still holding hands, looking into each other's eyes. The hum of other voices receded, replaced by the drumbeat of her pulse in her ears. She leaned toward him, lips parted, anticipating his kiss. Something in him told her he needed a woman like her, someone wild and unpredictable, to shake up his life. To show him how to really live. And she needed him, too, though she couldn't say why just yet. If only he'd give her the chance to find out.

CRAIG WAS seriously contemplating kissing Marlee when a tap on the shoulder saved him from what would probably have been a big mistake. "You folks look like you're ready to find a room." Mayor Hoskins nudged him and laughed. Judging by his flushed face and overly bright eyes, Craig guessed the mayor had had a few too many glasses of spiked punch.

Reluctantly, he followed his host off the dance floor. The last thing he needed right now was to be alone in a room with Marlee. His mind might look at things logically and understand why getting involved with her wasn't a good idea, but his body said "To hell with logic, let's go with emotion."

The mayor's wife, who was cheerily sober, drove them back to their home. While she and the mayor chatted about the festival and the dance, Craig and Marlee sat silent in the back seat. Marlee stared out the window. She acted put out with him, but why? Because he thought they should keep things casual? After all, the two of them hardly knew each other.

His body wasn't buying that excuse, either. It wasn't as if he hadn't had his share of one-night stands and brief flings before. But, as old-fashioned as it sounded, Marlee didn't strike him as that kind of girl. Despite her bohemian clothes and carefree attitude, she was small-town enough to revel in a strawberry festival, and let the mayor and his wife think they were married rather than embarrass herself.

The mayor showed them to their room, a small pink chamber filled with white and gold furniture: a dresser, nightstand and a double bed topped by a pink ruffled canopy. The bed looked surprisingly small and narrow. Intimate.

"Now if you need anything, our room is right down the hall." The mayor winked. "Oh, and the bed squeaks. Just thought I'd let you know."

Marlee blushed. She did that a lot. It was kind of cute. He'd never thought of himself as attracted to "cute" women before, but maybe that was because he hadn't been exposed to many. He'd dated women who were beautiful, sophisticated, elegant or even "striking," but never cute.

As soon as they were alone, he pulled the pink quilted coverlet off the bed and deposited it on the floor, along with a pillow. "I'll sleep here," he said.

She bit her lip, and he had the impression she was about to protest, but instead she grabbed up her smaller suitcase and turned toward the bathroom. "I'll get ready for bed."

IN THE BATHROOM, Marlee had a moment of feeling disoriented. Here she was, in a small town so much like the one where she'd been raised, in a house that was so much like her parents' suburban ranch. For a moment, when she looked in the mirror she halfway expected to see teenage Marlee, complete with acne and badly permed hair.

Thank God she'd improved with age, she thought

as she examined her face in the mirror. Not only had her skin cleared up and a good hairdresser worked wonders on her straight locks, but also she wasn't the same inside. Beyond the obvious improved judgment (she hoped!) and sense of perspective maturity had given her, she no longer had the small-town sensibilities she'd once possessed.

All right, some of that still existed. She hadn't been able to bring herself to correct Clara Hoskins when she'd referred to Craig as Marlee's husband. Maybe it was because Clara looked so much like her Aunt Betty, the Baptist minister's wife. Or maybe it was a more perverse side of Marlee that enjoyed sharing a private joke with Craig.

Not that he thought it was all that funny, but she'd certainly had to hold back giggles at the sight of his face when Clara had conferred an instant marriage license on him.

Beyond that, though, Marlee wasn't *comfortable* in this small-town world, the way she'd once been. Living in the city had changed her. She liked the excitement of the city, all the opportunities it offered, not to mention the privacy. Though there were more people in D.C. than in a place like Downieville or Dimitt, most of them were strangers. Marlee was able to do almost anything and not be judged for her actions.

Which brought her back to Craig and this crazy attraction between them. Obviously he felt it, too. So what were they going to do about it?

They were both away from home, away from family and jobs and anyone they knew. Why not make the most of the opportunity? Granted, ordinarily she'd never sleep with a man she'd met only that morning, but there was nothing ordinary about the past fourteen hours. Why not give herself permission

to have a fling with a man who was so unlike anyone she'd ever choose in her "real" life—but one who
turned her on, nonetheless?

The thought brought a rush of anticipation and a
feeling of, well, *power*. The small-town girl she'd once
been would never have dreamed of something like
this. The big-city woman she'd become couldn't wait
to give it a try!

CRAIG SAT on the edge of the bed and removed his
shoes, then stared at the closed bathroom door, trying—and failing—to keep from imagining Marlee
naked. He heard the shower running and tortured himself with fantasies of water sluicing over ivory skin—

"Aaargh!" With a groan, he stood, his back to the
door, and stripped off his shirt. His plan was to be
settled in for the night by the time she came out of
the bathroom. Asleep even, or at least pretending to
sleep, so there'd be no further discussion of the sleeping arrangements.

He hesitated before unzipping his pants. He
should have packed pajama bottoms or even gym
shorts. But he hadn't planned on sharing a room with
his passenger—all of the reservations he'd made had
been for two rooms. What the hell. It wasn't like
boxer shorts were that revealing.

Except when you had a hard-on that wouldn't
quit. He frowned at his obvious arousal, then tossed
his pants aside and lay down on the rug. He reached
up to switch off the lamp then pulled the bedspread
over himself. *Think about something else*, he told himself. *Something that has nothing to do with sex.*

Usually when he couldn't sleep, he wrote menus
in his head. Appetizers, entrées, side dishes and des-
serts for his restaurant. Crostini Napoletani, fresh-

corn-and-sausage fritters, quesadilla marina, salmon en papillote, apricot-stuffed chicken breasts, chicken marabella, honey-soy short ribs, pumpkin mousse, chocolate pots de crème...

The door to the bathroom opened, a shaft of light spotlighting him. "Oh, I'm sorry," Marlee squeaked.

He opened his eyes and stared at the lithe figure in the doorway. She wore a gauzy white gown which was made practically transparent by the light behind her. As Craig's tortured senses registered the full breasts, small waist and curvy hips, all thoughts of poultry and pastry fled from his brain. He closed his eyes again, pulled the cover up to his chin and lied through his teeth. "That's okay. You aren't disturbing me."

People in hell don't want ice water, either. And he had a bridge in Arizona he could sell her....

The room went dark and a few seconds later pain shot through him as her foot came in contact with his thigh. "Oh, I'm terribly sorry. I can't see anything." She scrambled over him, kicking him twice more in the process, and dove onto the bed, which squeaked wildly in protest.

Great. Mayor Hoskins probably thought they were going after it like rabbits. If only...

Think about food, he ordered himself. *How to prepare pork tenderloin Diane. First, cut pork tenderloin into one-inch medallions....*

This floor was hard as concrete. He'd be crippled by morning. He rolled over onto his side. Above him, the bed creaked again as Marlee shifted position. On their way out of town, maybe they'd buy the mayor and his wife a can of WD-40 as a thank-you present.

"Craig?"

"Yes?" He didn't even bother feigning sleep. What was the point?

"I was just wondering. Why don't you like me?"

"What makes you think I don't like you?"

"Oh, I don't really mean as a friend. But...you know."

He blinked. This was some of that girl-code he'd never been able to figure out. "Guess what I mean, even though my words don't make sense." Even harder to decipher with no physical cues. "Um, what exactly do you mean?"

"Well, it's obvious we're attracted to each other, but you don't seem to want to have sex with me."

Her choice of words hit him in the gut. Yes, he was attracted to her, and the problem wasn't that he didn't want to have sex with her. He'd have gladly had sex with her six ways to Sunday, if he was sure that was all it would be.

But any woman who would lie about being married in order to avoid embarrassing herself or her hosts was the type who would fall in love with a man she slept with. She wasn't one of the more experienced women he usually went for. She wasn't the type of woman who understood the difference between a romp between the sheets and happily ever after.

And the last thing he needed right now was a woman who thought she was in love with him. He sighed.

"What's that supposed to mean?" she asked. "It wasn't a stupid question."

"It's not that I don't find you attractive. Obviously, I do. But I think it's better if we keep things casual between us. Just friends. This isn't a good time in my life for a relationship." There, that made sense, didn't it? He'd told the truth and hadn't said anything to hurt her feelings.

"You mean you *plan* when to have a relationship? Like scheduling a dinner party or something?"

He frowned. Of course Miss Wake-up-in-a-new-world-every-day wouldn't understand. What was he thinking? "I'm busy getting my career on track," he said. "Once that's more settled, I can think about settling down with a woman who thinks the same way I do."

"What way is that? Boring?"

"You think I'm boring?"

She rolled over and looked down at him. In the dim light filtering through the curtains he could just make out her face—the hollows of her eyes, the curve of her cheek. Her lips looked soft, unsmiling but still so tempting....

"A boring man wouldn't dance the jitterbug," she said. "A boring man wouldn't pick watercress by a stream or walk out on a log over the water. A boring man wouldn't kiss me the way you kissed me. But I think you like to pretend you're boring."

He frowned. "Why would I do that?"

"Because it's safe. Because you think it's what's expected. You're not the only one. I see it all the time."

"Thank you, Ms. Freud."

She flopped onto her back once more. "Go ahead and make fun. But while you and all your perfectly correct clones are marching along to your five-year plans, people like me are really living." She rolled over, her back to him.

He wanted to say something else, to defend himself, but maybe she was right. Maybe he *was* boring. And safe. What was wrong with that? Maybe that was the best way to get ahead in life. The best way to have things that really mattered. What did she have? A dead-end job and a tacky apartment and no license. Was he wrong to want more than that?

In any case, he wasn't going to fight with her about this. He was the way he was and no woman would change him, no matter how much she turned him on. "I guess I'll put my boring self to sleep then," he said. "Say good-night, Marlee."

A muffled giggle drifted down to him. "Good night, Marlee."

He smiled, pleased with himself. A boring man wouldn't make her laugh like that, would he? He punched his pillow and closed his eyes, willing himself to sleep. They had a long day ahead tomorrow. A long week on the road. And, he hoped, no more detours.

5

WE'RE SOMEWHERE IN Tennessee. Miles of green rolling fields, blue skies, scenic beauty, etc. etc. So exciting I keep dozing off. I mean, when you've seen one cow, you've pretty much seen them all, right? Of course, there's always my traveling companion, the Chef, to keep me awake. A man of mystery in more ways than one. I will admit he's easy on the eyes, though he doesn't talk much. Typical male of the species. I'm determined to discover his secrets, though. Will keep you posted, faithful readers.

MARLEE SWITCHED OFF her laptop and shut the lid. She stretched her arms out in front of her and yawned. She definitely needed to do something to wake up.

"Looks like rain up ahead." Craig spoke for the first time in an hour, startling her.

She looked out the windshield at the gray clouds on the horizon. "That'll be a nice change. I love a good storm."

"You're not the one who has to drive in it. If the weather turns bad, it could really slow us down."

There he went with his precious schedule again. "It's not like we have to rush. We have plenty of time to get to San Diego."

His hands tightened on the steering wheel. "I

hoped we'd make West Memphis by nightfall. We have rooms booked."

"If we don't make it we'll find someplace else to stay. Maybe someplace interesting."

He shook his head. "Are you always so complacent?"

Are you always so superior? she thought. "I prefer to think of it as open to adventure." She shrugged. "It gives me stuff to write about."

He glanced at the laptop. "So people really read this Web diary of yours?"

"Yeah, they do." She stashed the laptop in the back seat. "Does that surprise you?"

"A little. Don't people have better things to do with their lives than read other people's diaries?"

"Apparently some people don't." She tucked one leg under and half-turned to face him. "It's merely another form of entertainment, like reading one of those old serials they used to run in the newspaper, or watching a soap opera on TV. People—or most people anyway—are interested in what others are doing."

"They're voyeurs."

Apparently not something straitlaced Craig approved of. But was he really so conservative? She leaned toward him and adopted a sexy purr. "Now what's so bad about being a voyeur?"

He glanced at her over the top of his sunglasses. "I guess it depends on what—or who—you're watching."

Bingo! The man was not as cool and reserved as he pretended to be. The trick now was to keep him warmed up and maybe make him drop his guard even more. If they were going to spend hours and hours in each other's company, they might as well have some fun. "Let's play a game," she said.

"You mean like trying to see who can spot the most different license plates?"

"I was thinking of something a little more interesting."

"Such as?"

She laughed at the worried look on his face. "How about a little Truth or Dare?"

"Isn't that something junior-high-school kids play?"

"It can be pretty interesting as an adult."

"I don't know." He frowned.

"Oh, come on. It'll be fun. We each come up with a question and the other person has to tell the truth, or they have to take a dare."

"How will you know if I'm telling the truth?"

"I'm very perceptive. I'll know." She was bluffing, of course, but he didn't know that. And after all, women's intuition had to be good for something, or people wouldn't talk about it so much. "You go first," she said. "Ask me if I want a truth or a dare."

He hesitated. She was about to accuse him of being a bad sport when he asked. "All right. Truth or dare?"

"Truth."

"What's your favorite meal?"

She laughed. "Leave it to you to ask about food. You need to ask something more challenging than that."

"No, I really want to know—what would be your perfect meal?"

She hugged her arms over her stomach and thought a moment, then said. "I'd want a comfort-food feast. Macaroni and cheese. Meat loaf. Green beans cooked with lots of bacon. Homegrown tomatoes. And finish it off with peach cobbler and ice cream. And don't forget the big glass of iced tea."

He laughed and shook his head.

"What? Not gourmet enough for you?"

"No, it sounds delicious. Terrible for your heart, but delicious."

"My heart is just fine, thank you very much." She stuck her tongue out at him.

"It's your turn to ask me."

"Truth or dare?"

"Truth."

"What was your most embarrassing moment?" There, she'd show him how the game was supposed to be played.

He shook his head. "I don't think I want to answer that."

"You have to. That's the whole point of the game."

"Says who?"

"Says everybody. Haven't you played this game before?"

He gave her a look that said he was above such silliness, but she didn't believe him. Hadn't he ever done anything light-hearted and ridiculous? If he hadn't, he had a lot to make up for. Making a fool of yourself every once in a while helped keep all the serious stuff of life in perspective.

"What if I refuse to answer?" he asked.

"Then I'll find a way to get back at you. I'll do something to you you won't like at all."

He laughed. "I'm scared now."

"I mean it." She glared at him. "I can be very vindictive when I want to be."

He shook his head, still half chuckling. "What would you do?"

"I don't know yet." She folded her arms and assumed a mysterious expression. "But you might wake up one morning and find your fingernails painted pink."

"How would you get into my room?"

Was he implying that he hadn't considered possibly inviting her in? The thought had certainly crossed *her* mind. "I have my ways," she said, chin up.

"You'll have to do better than that to scare me."

She thought a minute, staring out over the dash and trying to come up with something he'd consider dire enough to want to avoid. Her vision zeroed in on the hood ornament of the Beemer and a wicked smile reached her lips. "All right. Suppose you come out to the car one morning and discover molasses all over your steering wheel, and the windshield smeared with Vaseline."

He went pale. "You wouldn't!"

She laughed. "Why not? It's just a car."

He winced. "It is not *just* a car."

No, in her experience men considered their cars an extension of themselves. Even her boss, Gary, who professed to disdain Americans' dependence on gas-guzzling automobiles, had been caught carefully wiping smudges off the hood of his ten-year-old Volvo with a handkerchief. She leaned toward Craig. "Fess up or you won't recognize this baby by the time I'm through with it."

He glared out the front window. "What was the question again?"

"Your most embarrassing moment. What was it?"

He made a growling noise in his throat and muttered curses, which she was sure were directed at her. "Talent show my junior year of high school."

That was the best he could come up with? She sank back in the seat, disappointed. "What was so embarrassing about that?"

His knuckles whitened on the steering wheel. "I decided I would do a juggling act."

"You know how to juggle!" She clapped her hands together. "How cool."

"I thought I knew how to juggle. But when I got on that stage, I was so nervous I messed up and made a complete fool of myself."

"Oh, I'm sure it wasn't as bad as that."

He made a face. "It was pretty awful. I swore I'd never juggle again."

The pain in his voice made her chest hurt. "But that was a long time ago. I bet you could still juggle if you wanted."

"Not much call for it in my line of work."

"Still, I don't think it's all that embarrassing. Not like being caught naked in front of a bunch of co-eds, or up-chucking on your date's mom or something."

"Obviously my college days weren't as wild as yours. Or are you referring to recent events?"

"I was speaking metaphorically. At least I know how to have fun."

"Those sound like fun times all right."

She couldn't keep from laughing. She'd always been a sucker for sarcasm. "It's your turn."

"Truth or dare?"

She tilted her head, considering. "I think I'll go with dare."

He rolled his eyes. "You would."

"Come on. You have to think of a dare. And make it a good one."

"I'm thinking." The sun had been swallowed up in the clouds by now, so he took off his sunglasses and tucked them in the pocket of his shirt. "All right, I've got it. Recite the twelve times tables."

"What?" He had to be kidding.

"You heard me. The twelve times tables."

Where had he come up with that one? She sat up straight and attempted to look unconcerned. The sky was really dark now, and a few fat raindrops spattered the windshield. "Twelve times one is twelve. Twelve times two is twenty-four. Twelve times three..." She did great until she hit twelve times seven. "Twelve times seven is eighty-two."

"Wrong. Twelve times seven is eighty-four."

She leaned over and punched him in the arm. "How did you know I hate math?"

He laughed. "Let's just say you don't strike me as the analytical type."

"I don't know whether to be insulted or impressed by your perception."

"I vote for impressed."

She crossed her arms over her chest and fixed him with a mock glare. "All right, smarty pants, it's your turn. Truth or dare?"

The rain was falling harder now. He kept his eyes on the road. "Truth. No, wait—dare."

"Sing your school fight song."

"The Culinary Institute doesn't have a school fight song."

"Then sing your high-school fight song."

"I don't remember it." But the blush spreading up his neck betrayed him.

"I think you do remember."

He shook his head. "I don't."

"Either sing it, or sing 'I'm a Little Teapot.' *With* the hand motions."

"I'm driving."

She shrugged. "We can stop the car."

Rain was falling hard now, a steady drumbeat on the car roof. He didn't say anything for a long moment, then he groaned, and began to sing. "You've got to fight, fight, fight for the gold and blue. You've got to something, something, something and to your school be true."

It was more like croaking, actually. She refrained from putting her hands over her ears. "Stop, please," she said.

His grin was smug. He turned the wipers up a notch. "Truth or dare?"

"Truth."

"Your first sexual experience—who, when, where?"

Ah. Now things were getting interesting. "Tommy McIlhaney. I was fifteen, he was sixteen. At the end of Highline Road after the homecoming dance. I was pretty unimpressed."

"Tommy didn't make the earth move, huh?"

"The car shook a lot, but that's about it. It was all over with pretty quickly, as I recall. Too quickly."

"I trust your later experiences were more worthwhile."

"Oh, yes. I'd say things have improved greatly since I was fifteen." She grinned, enjoying the zing of sexual energy zipping between them. Sure, they might not intend to do anything about it, but she enjoyed the feeling all the same. "Truth or dare?" she asked.

"Truth."

"Describe *your* first sexual experience."

He was silent for a long moment, apparently thinking. Did he not remember? Had there been so many others since then he'd lost track? Or was he stalling?

"Meredith Simpson. I was sixteen, she was nineteen. Her parents' basement rec room one afternoon. I was *very* impressed."

Hmmm. That was good to know. Merely for curiosity's sake… "What made you decide to become a chef?"

"It's my turn. Besides, you didn't say 'truth or dare.'"

She tucked one leg under her again and settled more comfortably in her seat. "Game's over. Now we're just talking."

"So you're making the rules here."

She grinned. "Of course. The game was to break the ice. Now that the conversation's on a roll, we don't need it anymore."

"Aren't you the clever one?"

"Answer my question. Why did you decide to become a chef?"

"I like food. I enjoy cooking. But I like the business side of running a restaurant, too. There's always something happening, so it's never boring or routine." He shrugged. "And I like to be in charge."

"Obviously."

"What's that supposed to mean?"

"Nothing. You just strike me as the bossy type."

"Takes one to know one, I'd say."

"You're wrong there. In my job, I am no one's boss. But that's okay. When you're low on the totem pole, people leave you alone."

"What exactly is it that you do? I mean, I know you said you design ad campaigns, but what does that entail?"

"Ad campaigns for nonprofits. Reading Is Fundamental, Head Start, National Education Association, that sort of thing. Low budget, no glamour."

"But you love it."

"Well, yeah. Most of the time. I get to be creative, work with all kinds of artists and actors and teachers."

"But you didn't say you love it all the time. So what don't you like about the job?"

She shifted position, trying to get more comfortable. "Well, like I said, I'm pretty far down in the pecking order, so I don't get the best jobs. And the pay could be better, but there are other things more important than money. I mean, I'm making a real difference in people's lives."

"You think it's important to make a difference?"

"Of course! Look at you." She gestured to him. "The people who come into your dining room are doing important work. They could eat anything to keep going, but you give them good food to provide a pleasant break in their day."

He looked amused. "Cooking as a calling? I'll admit, I hadn't thought of it that way before."

"You should. Think how much our lives revolve around eating. Food is important."

"Speaking of food, what should we have for dinner?"

She looked out the window at the rain, which continued to fall in sheets, turning the pavement to a mirror which reflected back their headlights. "In this weather, comfort food." She leaned forward to get a better look ahead of them. "Look, up there. It's a Kuntry Kafé."

"I'm not sure I trust a place that spells *country* and *café* with a *K*."

"Aww, c'mon, live a little. You have to take more chances in life."

One eyebrow rose, mocking her. "Says who?"

"Says me. After all, you took a chance inviting me along on this trip. You might as well go for broke."

"When you put it that way…" He flipped on his blinker and turned into the parking lot of the Kuntry Kafé. He pulled into an empty space and switched off the engine. "Don't blame me if nothing here is edible."

"You worry too much."

"Maybe you don't worry enough."

"Then I'd say we're a perfect pair. We balance each other out." Her eyes met his, electricity sparking between them that had nothing to do with the lightning outside. Rain thundered around them, cool dampness seeping into the warm cocoon of the car. She had a flash of memory of that long-ago night on Highline Road. It had been raining then, too. There was something intimate about the interior of a car in the rain. They were closed off from the rest of the world, separated from everyday problems.

Not to mention it was a fine incubator for lust. She was close to suggesting they skip dinner and head straight for dessert, but before she could put the idea into words, he put his hand on the door latch. "We'd better make a run for it."

She studied the pouring rain. "We'll be soaked."

"That's okay. I'm hungry."

She was hungry, too, but not for peach cobbler. She sighed. Might as well eat now. She could always hope for dessert later. A certain handsome chef might be able to cook up something to please her.

CRAIG STUDIED Marlee as she sat across from him in the orange vinyl booth in the Kuntry Kafé dining room. Her hair was plastered to her forehead and water trickled down the side of her face. Moisture glittered on the tips of her lashes and sparkled on the fine hairs of her forearms. She reminded him of a wet kitten, though he was sure he'd never seen a kitten grin with such enthusiasm.

"Look, they have meat loaf and macaroni and cheese," she said as she studied the menu. "And peach cobbler."

"No homegrown tomatoes, though."

"Since this isn't my grandmother's house, I don't expect perfection." She closed the menu and laid it aside. "What about you? What are you going to have?"

"I guess I'll try the pot roast."

"I'll bet it's good."

He glanced around at the orange booths, orange and blue plaid curtains and the multitude of chicken figurines arranged by the cash register. "How can you tell?"

"It's pouring rain and the place is full. That's a good sign."

"Maybe there's no place else around here to eat."

"If that's the case, maybe you should move here and open your restaurant."

He picked up a chicken-shaped salt shaker and studied it. "I'm not sure I'm up to their standards."

A waitress named Reba who called him "hon" took their orders. Ten minutes later she returned, staggering under the weight of plates overflowing with food. Fragrant steam rose from the pot roast and gravy, green beans, mashed potatoes, macaroni and cheese, meat loaf and yellow squares of corn-bread. "I'm in heaven," Marlee said, before attacking her plate like a starving person.

He sampled the pot roast. Not bad. Quite good, actually. He watched Marlee as she inhaled meat loaf. She had a frightening enthusiasm for everything. Which led to thoughts of how she might go about satisfying other appetites.

He shook his head. Better not go there. The thing

to remember was that she was definitely not his type. Too flighty. Too unpredictable. Too guileless.

"How's your dinner?" she asked.

"Good." He stirred gravy into the mashed potatoes. "Better than I expected."

"That's because you're too cynical."

"Coming from you, that's not saying much."

"What's that supposed to mean?"

"I've never met such an obviously intelligent grown woman who was so amazingly naive."

She laid aside her fork, eyes narrowed. "What's that supposed to mean?"

He focused on cutting his pot roast into bite-sized pieces. "Just that your whole 'the world is a wonderful place and whatever happens is great' routine is too unreal. You can't go through your life that way, with no plan, no preparation for times when things go wrong. And they will go wrong. Depend upon it."

"So what if they do? Is being down in the mouth about it going to make things better?" She shoveled a forkful of macaroni into her mouth and chewed.

"I merely think it's better to be prepared."

"I have insurance. I have savings. After that, what more can you do?"

He frowned. She made it sound so simple. "Having a plan to fall back on doesn't hurt."

She shrugged. "If your mind's already made up about what you're going to do, you might miss out on a better alternative."

He finished the last of the roast and pointed his fork at her. "That's another thing—people like you are impossible to argue with."

She smiled, a Cheshire-cat grin. "And we love driving people like you crazy."

How could you stay angry with someone who refused to return the favor? He gave up and settled into polishing off the rest of the meal. When the waitress returned to take their plates, he even allowed Marlee to talk him into sharing her peach cobbler. The buttery crust and cinnamon-sweet peaches tasted heavenly, he had to admit.

"Feeling better?" she asked after they'd paid the bill and were walking toward the door.

"I feel fine."

"That's good. I've noticed men often get grouchy when their blood sugar drops."

"I am not grouchy," he protested.

There she went with the inscrutable smile again. "Of course not."

All right, so maybe he'd been a little tense, what with the weather and all. Thankfully, the rain had let up by the time they left the restaurant. "If we push it, we can make Savannah, Tennessee, tonight."

She stretched her arms over her head and arched her back, breasts thrust forward. He watched her out of the corner of his eye, mouth dry. Did she have any idea of the effect she had on him?

Her eyes met his and her smile this time was downright seductive. Busted! He turned away and fumbled with the car keys. "What's your hurry?" she all but purred. "We've got plenty of time."

Maybe she thought so, but as far as he was concerned, the sooner they reached California, the better. The more time he spent alone with Marlee, the more she messed with his head. So much for doing any serious thinking on this trip. So far all he could think about was her!

WE'VE COME to the end of day two of my travels with the Chef. No daring adventures to report today. He refused my suggestion that we stay at the Li'l Abner Motor Courts in Pulaski in favor of rooms at a standard Econo Inn outside of Savannah, Tennessee. Boring! Of course, it's the safe choice. The Chef isn't much of a gambler. He did, however, consent to dinner at the Kuntry Kafé, so he isn't a total stick-in-the-mud. Now if I could only wean him from his obsessive schedule....

6

DAY THREE dawned overcast and oppressively humid. Marlee cranked up both the air conditioner and the stereo in an attempt to make up for the depressing weather. She bopped in her seat as Stevie Ray wailed about it flooding down in Texas.

"Let's hope it doesn't flood in Tennessee." Craig cast a worried look at the darkening sky.

"If the weather gets too bad, we'll stop." She pointed to a billboard ahead. "We could visit Graceland and wait for the weather to clear. I've always wanted to go there."

His frown deepened. "I have no intention of stopping at Graceland. I was really hoping we could make up some time today. We're almost a full day behind schedule."

She rolled her eyes. "Do you have sex on a schedule, too?"

He glared at her, then jerked his eyes back to the road. "What kind of a crack is that?"

She leaned over and turned down the stereo. "You have everything else in your life planned out, I thought maybe you had a timetable for relationships, too. You know, 'August 31, 2006, find woman to marry. September 7, take intended to bed. December 20, buy engagement ring, etc., etc., etc.'" She faked a huge yawn.

His face was red, though whether from embarrassment or anger she couldn't tell. She shrank back a little, worried she might have taken things too far. Honestly, didn't he understand the concept of over-the-top humor?

"I suppose your philosophy involves something like flitting along, hither and yon, until you literally stumble over a man, with whom you then fall madly in love and into bed, and live happily ever after."

Laid out that way, the words dripping with sarcasm, such a "philosophy" sounded fatalistic and ridiculous. But yeah, he'd nailed her approach to relationships pretty well. "Last I checked, love is an emotion and emotions don't follow logic. No matter how much some people want them to."

He flinched. Aha. She'd scored a direct hit. She relaxed a little, and turned toward him. "Why don't we agree that you and I have two different approaches to life? For the sake of sanity on this trip, maybe we could try to meet in the middle."

He looked wary. "What do you consider 'the middle'?"

She tucked her legs up under her and considered for a moment. "How about I don't rag on you so much about your schedule, and you try to loosen up a little and not get bent out of shape if things don't go as planned."

"I could definitely go for that first part." He nodded. "And despite what you think, I *do* know how to cut loose—when it's appropriate."

"Then we'll have to make sure and find an appropriate time." She grinned. "This, I'd like to see. And hey, maybe I can try your logical, organized approach to something. Though it will probably make my head hurt."

He laughed. "Truce?"

"Truce." She leaned forward and kissed him on the cheek.

"Hey, what was that for?" His face had a decidedly pink tinge.

"Well, I couldn't shake your hand while you're driving, so I sealed our bargain with a kiss." She settled back in the seat, a pleasant warmth humming through her veins. Her lips on his cheek had brought back memories of the *real* kiss they'd shared by the creek. The chemistry between them was definitely still there. Amazing as it sounded, she had the hots for Mr. Uptight and Organized. And if her intuition was right, he was attracted to her, too. Was that wild, or what?

THEY DROVE through intermittent rain all day. Craig had to concede all hope of keeping to his schedule was lost. He was surprised how much better he felt once he admitted that to himself.

Or maybe it was his passenger who was responsible for his new attitude. Was it possible her come-what-may approach was rubbing off on him? He couldn't deny he found her sometimes wacky view of the world entertaining. Having her along made the miles go faster and the bad weather easier to deal with.

"I think it's getting worse out there." She leaned forward to study the thickening curtain of rain surrounding them.

"Yeah. I don't want to try to drive in this after dark," he admitted. It would be easy to miss a turn-off in this kind of weather and the last thing he wanted was to end up lost with the queen of misdirection. She'd have the whole world laughing at him once she posted the tale on her Web site.

"Where are we, anyway?" she asked.

"Outside of West Memphis, Arkansas." He checked the gas gauge. "I need to stop for gas soon."

She leaned over to peer at the fuel-level indicator. "You still have almost half a tank."

"I don't like to let it get too low, especially in this kind of weather."

"Aw, come on. Let it go to at least a quarter tank. Live dangerously."

She was teasing him, he knew. "Go ahead and make fun," he said. "I know you think I'm uptight, but I've accomplished a lot so far."

"And I haven't." She sat back in her seat, the lightness gone from her voice.

"I didn't say that." He risked a glance at her. "It's not like you're a bum on the street. And unlike *some* people, I don't expect everyone to live by the same rules I do."

"I'm not sure I believe in living by rules, except maybe the golden one."

The idea was both alarming and attractive. What would it be like to approach life with no restrictions? "I seem to remember we agreed to try to meet each other halfway on this, so I'll wait to fill the tank. Meanwhile, see if you can spot a decent place to eat."

"By decent, I suppose you mean conventional?"

"Let's settle for edible."

"Now *that* sounds like an excellent idea."

While Johnny Lang crooned about the woman who stole his heart, Craig searched for a place to stop. He needed to get out and walk around, to work off some of his excess energy and get his mind off the woman who sat less than an arm's length away.

Fifteen minutes later, Marlee spotted a sandwich shop. "Does that meet your standards?" she asked.

"It'll have to do," he said, turning in. "I don't know if we'll find anything else before we reach Missouri."

They bought subs and ate them at a Formica table beside the window, rain so loud against the metal siding of the building they had to raise their voices to be heard. "I think we should find a place to stop for the night," she said.

"We're still two hours from Missouri," he said.

"It'll still be there in the morning, I'm sure."

He glared at her, but she only grinned more.

"So we'll spend the night in Arkansas," she said.

"I don't know if there are any hotels around here."

"We can look for one."

If anything, the rain was coming down harder when they started out again. By the time he got the car unlocked and they climbed in, they were both soaked. He switched on the heater before backing out of the parking lot. The headlights barely pierced the onslaught, and the pavement was slick with running water. He had to concentrate to keep the car on the road.

Lightning flashed, illuminating the nearly deserted highway. Thunder cracked. Marlee squeaked in alarm. "This is crazy," she said. "We should stop."

"And just where would you suggest we stop?" He hunched toward the dash, both hands locked around the steering wheel. "I don't see any motels, do you?"

"We'll stop at the first place we come to."

"Fine."

They said nothing for the next half hour, the wipers beating out a stupefying rhythm beneath the monotonous drumming of rain. He was lulled into a trance, every sense focused on the faintly discernable dashed line marking his lane and the short stretch of black pavement illuminated by his headlights.

"There!"

He jumped at Marlee's cry, heart pounding. "What?" he snapped.

"Up ahead. There's a motel."

The red neon vacancy sign flickered weakly through the veil of rain. Above that, in brighter blue light, the name Hiawatha Courts, complete with a blinking illuminated canoe, beckoned. He slowed at the entrance and stared at the long stone building, each door painted a different primary color. He shook his head. "You can't be serious."

"Why not? It looks clean. And it's the only place around."

"Maybe if we drive farther…"

"No." Her grip on his arm was surprisingly strong. "Don't be so stubborn. It's not safe."

The real fear in her eyes decided him. That, and the pincer-like pain at the back of his neck. He pulled forward beneath the portico, then went inside and rang the bell at the front desk. After a minute or so a heavy-set older woman emerged from a back room, followed by an older man. "Terrible night to be out," she said pleasantly.

"Yes. I saw your vacancy sign."

"You're in luck," the man said. "We got one room left." He pushed a pad of registration forms toward Craig. "Thirty-nine dollars plus tax."

"Only one room?" Of course. Why hadn't he seen that one coming? Not that he normally considered himself paranoid, but he couldn't help thinking fate was out to push all his buttons on this trip.

The woman nodded. "It's real nice. Queen-size bed, color TV with cable."

He shook his head. "Maybe I'd better try some-place else." He backed toward the door, but the man's voice stopped him.

"Next closest place is twenty-six miles. You don't want to drive that far in this weather. There's a tor-nado warning."

He glanced out the window at the car. Marlee sat slumped against the window. She looked as ex-hausted as he felt. He sighed. Fine. He'd survived one night in a room with her. He could survive an-other. "All right. I'll take it."

He didn't say anything when he went back out, merely handed her the room key and drove around to the side. "Where's your room?" she asked as he shut off the engine.

"They only had one." He unfastened his seat belt. "I can sleep in the car."

"Don't be ridiculous." She leaned into the back seat and picked up her tote bag, the one with her "emergency" supplies. "Come inside where you'll be warm and dry."

"No, really, I'll be fine. The seat reclines." He pulled the lever on the side of the driver's seat, send-ing the seat back to a forty-five degree angle.

"You'll be crippled if you try to sleep like that. Be-sides, it isn't safe."

He looked out at the sheeting rain. "I don't think a lot of muggers are out in weather like this."

She shoved the tote bag at him and reached for her computer. "Come inside."

Since he didn't really want to attempt to spend the night in the car, he followed her into the room. It was basic motel kitsch—Danish modern furniture, quilted chintz spread. A coffeemaker and packets of coffee sat on a table by the window.

"Look, a queen-size bed." She tossed her purse onto the end of the bed and set her laptop on the desk.

"I'll take the floor." He frowned at the braided rug beside the bed. It didn't look very comfortable.

"No, you took the floor the other night. I'll sleep there tonight."

His aching body and sleep-deprived brain refused to play the gentleman. "All right," he said, and walked past her into the bathroom.

When he came out, she'd changed into her night-clothes and was busy making a nest on the rug beside the bed. Every extra pillow and blanket was piled there, leaving him with a single coverlet and one pillow. "There, that should be pretty comfort-able," she said, smiling up at him.

Tired as he was, he still registered how perfectly adorable she was. He had an insane urge to curl up beside her and lay his head on her breast.

His eyes were already drifting closed on this pleas-ant thought when lightning bathed the room in bril-liant light. It had scarcely faded before thunder crashed and the room was plunged into darkness.

Marlee's scream still echoed in his ears as she scrambled into bed beside him, dragging blankets and pillows with her. She clung to him, shaking. "I r-really d-don't like thunder," she stammered.

She fitted in his arms so well. Her head nested perfectly in the hollow of his shoulder. His hand was the perfect size to cup *her* shoulder. She was soft and warm and her hair smelled like peaches. Suddenly, he wasn't so tired anymore, and he couldn't think of a single reason not to kiss her.

Marlee wasn't quite sure how she'd ended up in bed with Craig. The lightning and thunder had propelled

her off the floor in search of safety. The safest place
at the moment seemed to be Craig's strong arms.

Once there, she couldn't think of a single reason
to leave. After all, their bodies had been sending
tempting telegrams to each other for three days. And
she had that whole box of condoms she'd packed in
a moment of extreme optimism. Maybe she'd been
clairvoyant.

She smiled even as she snuggled closer and his
lips found hers. The man could kiss. Somewhere in
between making all his plans for the future and arranging his life just so, he'd managed to learn his way
around a woman's lips.

A knock on the door made them both freeze.
"Hello. Are you all right in there?"

"Who is that?" she whispered to Craig.

"I think it's the lady who runs this place. I guess
she and her husband are the owners." He raised his
head. "We're fine," he called.

"I brought you some candles. And an extra blanket. Lightning hit a transformer and the power's
going to be out a while."

"Just a minute." He leaned over, groping on the
floor for his pants.

"That's all right. I have my key." The door opened
and the thin beam of a flashlight arced across the
room. It settled on Marlee's face. She squinted at the
glare and saw a short, round woman who reminded
her of her Aunt Edna.

"Hello, dear," the woman said. She shuffled across
the room, to the bedside table, seemingly undis-
turbed that she'd found them in bed. "I thought you
and your husband might need a little extra light to
find your way around. I'll set the candles over here."

A match hissed and then the warm glow from the

fat taper in a pewter holder cast its glow around the bed. "There, that's better, isn't it?" She smiled. "And I brought you another blanket. This storm has put a real chill in the air." She unfurled the coverlet and it floated down over them. Marlee half expected her to lean over and tuck in the edges. Instead, she stepped back toward the door. "I'll leave you alone now," she said, still smiling. "It's an inconvenience, I know, but I must say, there's something so romantic about a blackout, don't you think?"

Then she was gone, the door shutting firmly behind her. Marlee looked at Craig. "She thinks we're married."

"I guess so."

Funny how there was a lot of that going around. Did she and Craig really look like a couple? She rolled over to face him. The candlelight flickered over his face, accenting the fine bones of his cheeks, deepening the hollows of his eyes. She traced the curve of his nose with one finger.

"What are you thinking?" he asked.

"I'm thinking I'd like you to kiss me again."

There was a lot to be said for a man who could take a hint. In no time at all, he was kissing not only her mouth, but her neck, shoulders, breasts, and was working his way south. She arched her back and let out a sigh of pure contentment. She could think of a lot worse places to be than a cozy inn during a thunderstorm, making love by candlelight with a handsome man.

"Are you sure this is a good idea?" He paused, one hand on the top button of her nightgown.

"I think it's a very good idea." She pulled his head down for another sample of his smooching prowess. Every nerve in her body jumped up and down for joy.

It was a wonder all the tension that had been building for the past two days didn't make a hissing sound as it was released.

Except, of course, that another kind of tension was building as Craig got acquainted in a whole new way with her body and she set about exploring his. For a man who made his living in the kitchen, he certainly had a lot of nice hard muscles. To think she'd never realized all the benefits of working out before. Maybe in the future, she'd spend more time at the gym. If only to enjoy the scenery.

"I have some condoms in my bag," she said when they were both naked.

"Ah. The 'emergency supplies.'"

"I was never a Girl Scout, but I do know how to be prepared."

"I think the Boy Scouts are the ones with the 'Be Prepared' motto," he said, as he climbed out of bed and made his way to her bag.

"I probably would have had more fun in the Boy Scouts anyway." She sat up to get a better look. Candlelight on naked man. Mmmm, mmmm, mmmm.

He found the box of condoms and returned to bed. "Now where were we?"

"Here… And here…"

She slid down beneath the covers, oblivious now to the storm raging outside, every sense tuned to making her own brand of thunder and lightning.

"Yes, that's nice…. Very nice."

7

FROM NOW ON, my traveling companion will be known as the Magic Chef. Say no more...

CRAIG WOKE sometime the next morning in a tangle of sheets. Marlee lay on her back beside him, a single lock of hair across her face, the strands stirring each time she exhaled. He rose on one elbow and watched her. Her mouth was curved in a half smile. What had caused that smile? Thoughts of him, perhaps?

Recalling the events of the night before put a smile on his own face. He slid his hand over to cover her bare breast. She was so wonderfully soft and warm....

She opened one eye and stared at him. "Is it morning?"

"It's morning." He continued his explorations.

She rolled onto her side, spooning against him. "Is it raining?" she asked.

He glanced toward the front window. A bar of bright light showed at the gap in the curtains. "Looks like the sun's out."

"That's nice." She snuggled closer, her voice muffled by the pillow.

He squeezed her in a hug. "What do you want for breakfast?"

"A honey bun."

He thought at first this might be some sexual reference, then realized she was probably referring to the plastic-wrapped pastry commonly sold at convenience stores. "Why would you want one of those? Don't you know they have enough preservatives shot into them that they'll keep indefinitely?"

"I like them. A honey bun and a big cup of coffee. With sugar and cream."

He made a face. "How can you eat that stuff?"

Groaning, she flipped onto her back again. "What do *you* want for breakfast?"

"I was thinking a Denver omelette. Maybe some wheat toast. Black coffee."

"Fine. You want protein in the morning. Sugar and caffeine get me going."

"Speaking of sugar getting me going..." He slid further down in bed. "Maybe I'm not ready to head out to breakfast just yet...."

Sometime later, after Marlee had uploaded her latest blog entry, showered and repacked, they found themselves at a red-roofed establishment known as the Dutch Delight Diner. "I feel like I've stumbled onto the 'It's a Small World' ride at Disney," Craig said as he eyed the row of Dutch dolls staring down at him from a shelf above their table.

"I think it's cute." Marlee studied the menu as the waitress approached. "Look, they have homemade cinnamon rolls."

He grunted and ordered a Denver omelette. At least she hadn't talked him into breakfast at the 7-Eleven. "Do you have our schedule in your purse?" he asked. "I want to see if I can make up some lost time."

She added another packet of sugar to her coffee and shook her head. "I thought you were going to relax and forget about the schedule."

Had he said that? "I only meant that I accepted the fact that we were behind. That doesn't mean we can't get back on track now."

"What difference does it make if we're already behind?"

He ground his teeth together. "It means we add one day to my calculations and pick up from there."

She shook her head. "We can't do it."

"What do you mean we can't do it? Of course we can. We'll simply find our place on the schedule and pick up from there." They'd make the stops he'd planned for, only a day later. He'd breathe easier knowing things were going according to plan once more.

"We can't do it because I threw it out."

"You what?" He stared at her.

"I threw the schedule away." She shrugged. "I figured it was pretty well shot anyway."

"I made that schedule. You didn't have any right to throw it away." Some part of him knew he sounded a little irrational. It didn't make sense that his heart was pounding this way, either.

Marlee, on the other hand, looked as calm as if she'd just gotten a massage. She smiled at him pleasantly. "I think it'll be more fun to take our time, maybe visit a few tourist attractions on the way. We have plenty of time to get to the wedding."

"You want to visit tourist attractions?"

She dug in her purse and pulled out a handful of flyers. "I picked up a few brochures in the motel lobby this morning." She fanned the papers across the table between them. "The Wizard of Oz Museum is in Liberal, Kansas, only a couple of hours from here."

He stared at the brochure, which proclaimed in bright pink letters Have an Oz-Some Time! "The Wizard of Oz Museum?"

"It was my favorite movie when I was growing up. I'd love to see it."

He nodded, numb. Munchkins, Dorothy and the Wicked Witch of the West. Not exactly his idea of riveting entertainment. But he had a feeling he'd end up there anyway. Now that he'd slept with Marlee, she had at least a temporary hold on him. In the first throes of lust, the decision-making center of his brain had temporarily relocated to points south. That was one reason he tended to avoid all but the most superficial entanglements.

But there was no avoiding Marlee. The woman was a force unto herself. And one he wasn't particularly interested in resisting. At least for the moment. "Sure." He was surprised at how cheerful he sounded. "Let's follow the yellow brick road to Oz."

THE TINNY rendition of "Girls Just Wanna Have Fun" interrupted Marlee's lazy daydreaming. "What is that?" Craig asked as the car sped towards Liberal, Kansas.

"My phone." She groped through her totebag for the phone, which had been blissfully silent since they'd left D.C. "Hello?"

"What exactly do you mean by 'Magic Chef'? What is going on with you two?"

Marlee glanced at Craig, who watched her out of the corner of his eye. She smiled at him, she hoped reassuringly. "Uh, hi, Susan. Yes, everything is going fine so far."

"More than fine by the sound of things. But are you crazy?"

"Oh, you don't have to worry about us. We had a little bad weather, but it's beautiful now." She continued smiling inanely at Craig.

"I *am* worried about you. Craig Brinkman is *so* not your type."

"How do you know that?" she asked, her fake cheeriness slipping.

"I met the man a few times, you know. He's talented, driven and the kind of man who color-codes his closets and alphabetizes CDs."

She didn't know about the closet, but Susan had him nailed on the CDs. He wasn't going to be too thrilled when he saw how she'd disorganized them. "And your point is?" she asked.

"My point is, you couldn't have found a man less like yourself if you'd looked all over D.C."

"I know that." She was back to fake cheerfulness, though she was doing a slow burn inside. Why hadn't she remembered about Susan's unshakeable belief in her matchmaking abilities? "We're having a great time," she said. "A fun, relaxing trip. Today we're going to the Wizard of Oz Museum."

"You're what?"

She pulled the phone away from her ear, alarmed by the shrillness of Susan's tone. "They have Dorothy's house and a museum with scenes from the movie."

"I can't wait," Craig mumbled.

"I can't believe you talked Craig into that," Susan said. "You two must have really hit it off."

"Don't be silly." Yes, they'd hit it off all right. But it was only a fling. A fun diversion for the duration of the trip. Another adventure along the way. "We'll be there in plenty of time for your wedding."

"He's listening, isn't he? Well, I don't want you to get hurt. You're always getting involved with guys who are wrong for you and it never works out."

"Guys like the accordion player."

"You didn't even give him a chance."

"Never mind that. This is just for fun. We needed a break and decided to play tourist."

"As long as all you're doing is playing. Still, be careful."

"We will. Talk to you later." She clicked off before Susan could offer any more advice. Sheesh. As if she didn't know how to look after herself. She might be a little scattered sometimes, but she knew not to take things too seriously with a man like Craig.

"What was all that about?" he asked.

"Oh, she saw on the news about the bad weather and was checking on us." Amazing how easily the lie slipped off her tongue. She only hoped her face wasn't as red as it felt.

"What did she think about our detour to Oz?"

"Oh. She thought it was a great idea. Exactly what we both needed."

Of course it was a great idea. Not every destination—or every relationship—had to be serious.

The fact that she couldn't remember the last serious relationship she'd had didn't make any difference. She'd find the right man one of these days. She'd always assumed she'd stumble across him when the time was right, the way she always happened upon a gas station when she was almost out of gas, or a street sign when she was sure she was hopelessly lost. Life worked out that way, if you kept your eyes open and paid attention.

Mr. Right was out there somewhere. In the meantime, she could enjoy Mr. Right Now. Mr. Craig Brinkman.

And in the future, she'd be more careful about what she wrote in her blog....

A SIGN on the outskirts of Liberal, Kansas proclaimed it as the Gateway to the Land of Oz. Highway 59 into town was the Yellow Brick Road.

Marlee couldn't help thinking she was on her own personal search for the Emerald City. She'd promised herself she was going to use this trip to figure out what direction she should head next in her life, though to be perfectly honest, she hadn't done a great deal of thinking on the matter.

What quality would she ask the Wizard to give her—courage, heart, brains? Or maybe a sense of direction? She glanced at Craig, who was concentrating on watching for their turn. Since their detour to Downieville he'd refused all offers to let her take the wheel. She guessed she couldn't blame him. She'd been a little surprised he'd agreed to this side trip. There was hope for Mr. Anal yet.

He'd been anything but uptight last night. She smiled, remembering. As far as she was concerned, the evening ranked as one of the best of her life. She and Craig had been really good together. He'd been that rare specimen—at least based on her previous experience—a man who could take direction. So what was going to happen with them now?

Don't get ahead of yourself. You've gotten this far in life taking things one day at a time. That seemed as good an approach for this relationship as any.

"Tell me if you see a sign for Dorothy's house," Craig said, pulling her from her daydreams.

"Okay." She sat up straighter and concentrated on the passing scenery. "Too bad in real life the roads aren't color-coded. It would make things so much easier to find."

He stared at her. "Where do you come up with this stuff?"

She laughed. "It's called imagination."

"Uh-huh. Guess I was in a different line when they handed out that one. Wait, there's the sign." He put on his blinker and changed lanes.

"I don't know. You seemed pretty…inventive last night."

He grinned. "Maybe you inspire me."

A thrill shot through her at the words. She'd never been accused of being anyone's inspiration before. She reached over and squeezed his arm. "I'll bet you really are creative. You create new recipes and design menus, right?"

"Yeah. But that's my job."

"It's still creative."

"So in the kitchen I'm creative." He gave her a heated glance. "And in the bedroom. But elsewhere I consider myself more practical."

"And I'm not practical at all."

"Hey, I didn't say anything."

"I told you, I can read minds. Besides, I take it as a compliment." She smoothed her skirt across her knees. So what if he thought her flighty, unpredictable, even irresponsible? She'd heard all the criticism before. She knew refusing to plan too far ahead, to schedule her days to the last second and to make decisions based on goals went contrary to the way most people lived. She'd stopped expecting other people to approve of her years ago. Still, if she was being perfectly honest, she had to admit it stung a little to think Craig might look down his nose at her.

"Here we are. Dorothy's House and the Wizard of Oz complex." He turned into the parking lot. "Let's see what the Wicked Witch is up to these days."

They paid their admission to the complex and a woman dressed as Dorothy, complete with a blue gingham dress, pigtails and ruby-red slippers, greeted them to take them on a tour. "Our first stop is a replica of Dorothy's house as depicted in the 1939 film *The Wizard of Oz*," she announced.

Craig leaned over and whispered to Marlee, "I don't know—a grown woman dressed like that, it's kind of kinky."

She elbowed him in the ribs and followed the guide through the little gray farmhouse with the trapdoor in the middle of the floor that led to the cyclone cellar. "You should plan to come back in October," "Dorothy" said. "You can sign up to have breakfast with a Munchkin, and meet L. Frank Baum's great-great-grandnephew."

"It would be a shame to miss that," Craig said with a perfectly straight face.

They exited the back of the house and emerged on the yellow brick road. "Follow this road for a walk through the events of the movie," the guide said. "You'll meet the Scarecrow, the Tin Man, the Cowardly Lion and all the other characters we know and love."

"I wouldn't say all of us know and love them," Craig whispered.

Marlee made a face at him and led the way toward the Emerald City.

The yellow brick road wound among displays of mannequins set up to recall scenes from the famous movie. "Toto, I don't think we're in Kansas anymore," the Dorothy mannequin said, turning her head to survey her surroundings.

"And I've obviously been in Kansas too long," Craig muttered. "I can't believe I let you talk me into this."

"Come on, it's not so bad." She studied a mannequin of the Wicked Witch, it's animatronic face cackling wildly. "I'll get you, my pretty!"

"Aaack!" She screamed and clung to Craig as something buzzed her head.

"Relax." He laughed and pointed to the retreating figure. "It's only a winged monkey. A robotic one, I guess."

She shuddered. "I had nightmares for weeks about those things the first time I saw the movie."

He grinned. "And I always thought they were the coolest part."

They moved on, past singing Munchkins and talking trees, on to the Emerald City itself, where Dorothy and her cohorts gathered in a balloon that proclaimed "Spirit of Liberal, Kansas."

They ended up in the gift shop. "Imagine that," Craig said.

"Stop playing the bitter cynic. You know it wasn't so bad."

"I guess not. At least it got me out of the car to walk around for a while."

"You know I'll be happy to take my turn driving."

"Thanks, but I don't want to end up in Canada."

She stuck her tongue out at him, then stopped beside a display of Tin Man figurines. "We need one of these for the car."

"No thanks. I don't play with dolls."

"It's not a doll, it's an air freshener." She turned it over and opened a compartment on the back. "See, it's filled with potpourri."

"If I only had a heart—full of potpourri."

"Very funny." But she returned the Tin Man to the shelf and they moved one.

They looked at coffee mugs and refrigerator magnets, stuffed dolls and T-shirts. She stopped at a shelf of children's games and clapped her hands in delight. "We have to get these." She held up a small net bag of juggling balls attached to a book, *Learn to Juggle*.

"Thinking of taking up a hobby?"

"No, doofus, they're for you. So you can practice your juggling."

He took a step back. "I don't have any desire to practice my juggling."

"Oh, come on. You aren't seriously going to let one embarrassing moment years ago keep you from doing something you enjoy, are you?"

"Who said I enjoyed it?"

"Why did you take it up in the first place if you didn't enjoy it?" She clutched the bag to her chest. "I'm buying these. As a gift for you."

"Save your money."

"It's my money and I'm getting these for you. Think what a great stress reliever juggling could be. Or an icebreaker at your restaurant."

"The juggling chef. People will come from miles to see that."

She laughed and carried the juggling kit to the register. A few seconds later, he took his place in line behind her. "What are you buying?" she asked.

He held up the Tin Man air freshener. "A present for you. I thought maybe it was a subtle hint that I was stinking up the car."

She stood on tiptoe and kissed his cheek. "You're not as cynical as you like to pretend, you know that?"

He checked on either side of them, then spoke out of the side of his mouth. "Shhhh. You'll blow my cover."

They had lunch at Glynda's Goodies. He examined the collection of framed movie stills that filled the wall over their booth. A flying monkey grinned wildly at him at eye level. He supposed it could be worse. She might have insisted on eating only fast food. "What is it with you and the oddball diners and motels?" he asked.

"What do you mean?" She looked up from her Dorothy's Delight chef salad.

He sampled his Scarecrow's grilled chicken. Not bad. Maybe a hint too much garlic for his taste, but not bad. "I mean, is it some particular affection you have for kitsch, or is it a political statement, you know, a protest against corporate chains?"

She tilted her head, considering this. "I suppose those things are part of it," she said. "Mostly I like them because they're one of a kind." She took a long sip of cherry limeade. "That's what your restaurant should be. Eating out should be a real experience."

"I know that. But I'm not going to have some wacky theme restaurant." He made a face at the monkey.

"I'm not talking about theme. But something special. Think about who makes the reservations."

"What do you mean?"

"Most of the time the woman chooses the restaurant."

He nodded. "I won't argue with that."

"The way our society is set up, most men need a wife to balance out their lives. Wives are the ones who plan things, offer variety, etc."

"Isn't that a sexist thing to say?"

"I guess it's not very politically correct, and I'm not saying it applies to everyone, or even that it's right. But it's what I've seen over and over again. Think about it. Studies have proven that married men live longer than single men."

"Maybe it only seems like it. What about married women?"

"Single women live longer."

"So if single women live longer, but men need a wife, where does that leave them?"

"Sounds like gay men have the advantage."

"Well, I can tell you I certainly don't need a wife right now." Just in case she was getting any ideas. Not that she wasn't a nice person. She would probably make some carefree, directionally challenged man the perfect mate someday. "I'm perfectly capable of making my own dinner reservations and I don't need a woman to plan my social life."

"That's because you don't have one. A social life, I mean."

"How do you know that?" He didn't have much of a social life right now, but he certainly could, any time he wanted.

"I'm only guessing, but it sounds to me like all you ever do is work."

"That's not all I do. Besides, I enjoy my work." It was important to work hard now so that he'd be set in the future. If things went the way he planned, he'd have time for more leisure later. Why was she analyzing his life anyway?

He leaned toward her. "Besides, you're the one who needs someone to organize your life. You need someone to keep you from getting lost."

She sat up straighter, cheeks flushed, chin in the air. "I happen to enjoy the adventures I've had when I take a less than direct route to a destination."

He might have bought the whole offended dignity act if he hadn't glimpsed the real hurt in her eyes. He immediately felt like a heel. "Look, I didn't really mean you needed a keeper." Though he had to fight back an almost overwhelming urge to...to protect her. Despite her professed willingness to roll with the punches and embrace adventure, she had a certain vulnerability about her. He didn't like the thought of her out there, who-knows-where, all alone.

And now she stared at him with those enormous brown eyes of hers and he didn't know whether to grovel and apologize or kiss her.

Neither of which was possible right now anyway—the groveling because it was against his nature and the kissing because the table was between them. "It's none of my business anyway," he muttered.

"You're forgiven." She pushed aside her plate and lifted her laptop onto the table and opened it.

"Another update for your fans?" He asked. He was curious to know what she'd said about last night, if anything. Surely she wouldn't share something that personal with a bunch of strangers. But from what he could tell, she didn't keep much close to her chest.

"I want to write about the museum while it's still fresh in my mind." She stared at the screen a moment and started typing. "What was your favorite part of the museum?" she asked.

"At the end, where it said 'Exit.'"

"Mine was the gift shop. I mean, where else could you find a Tin Man air freshener?"

"No car should be without one."

Her fingers flew over the keys. He sat back, enjoying the opportunity to observe her while she was distracted by something else. A lock of hair had fallen across her left eye and she caught her bottom lip between her teeth as she studied the computer screen. She struck him as someone who put herself one hundred percent into whatever she did, whether it was writing a blog entry or making love.

He could relate to that. Sometimes when he experimented with a new recipe or designed a menu, he forgot himself and lost all track of time. And last night she had certainly had all of his attention.

"Why are you smiling at me like that?"

"Like what?" He hadn't even realized he was smiling.

"Like you're starving and I'm on the menu."

"That could be arranged." He leaned toward her and lowered his voice. "I don't think you'll have any trouble convincing me to turn in early tonight."

She turned pink. "Then if we're going to make any progress today, we'd better hit the road."

She started to close the laptop, but he put out his hand to stop her. "I want to hear what you wrote."

She hesitated, then cleared her throat. "All right. But it's not very exciting."

He sat back. "I'll be the judge of that."

"I convinced the Magic Chef to make a detour to the Wizard of Oz Museum in Liberal, Kansas, where we followed the Yellow Brick Road through scenes from the movie. Though the charm of Oz was lost on my practical pilot, he was a good sport. As a reward, I presented him with a gift of juggling balls. Apparently, dear friends, juggling is one of the Chef's many hidden talents! I told him he should use it as a draw for his restaurant, but he was less than thrilled with the idea.

Did I mention the Chef intends to open a restaurant? Though he hasn't been able to resist poking fun at some of my meal-time choices on this journey, I did get him to agree that dining should be a unique and entertaining experience.

So I'm opening it up to a reader poll. What kind of restaurant do you think the Magic Chef should open?"

She looked at him over the top of the computer. He stared back, open-mouthed. "Magic Chef?"

"Well, I couldn't use your real name." She grinned. "Before last night it was just 'the Chef.'"

He pointed to the computer. "You didn't write about us...I mean, you didn't tell them that we..."

"Of course not!" She shut the computer, clicking the top firmly closed. "I decided to change the name for myself."

That was something, at least. But he still didn't like the idea of being mentioned in her blog at all. "I haven't told very many people about my plans to open the restaurant. I mean, nothing's set in stone yet."

"That's all right. No one will know who you are. And it's not likely any of the people you hang out with even read blogs, much less mine."

"Are you saying the people I hang out with aren't cool enough to read blogs?"

"It's not really a matter of cool." She studied him a moment. "Let's just say it's more a matter of being conservative and mainstream. Like you." With that, she slid out of the booth and led the way out of the restaurant.

He followed. What was so wrong with being conservative and mainstream? She made it sound like he was lacking something.

Then again, she *had* dubbed him "Magic."

YES, IT'S ME AGAIN, *trying to fight the boredom of cruising across Kansas. I'm sure there are many wonderful people in this state, but the view from the car is a cure for insomnia. So once again I turn to you, dear readers, for solace and entertainment.*

   The Magic Chef was embarrassed to learn he's being discussed in this blog, no matter how anony-

mously. In fact, he's sending me worried looks at this very moment, wondering what I'm putting in here about him. I just smile at him mysteriously over the top of the computer screen and keep typing. A little mystery never hurt a woman's reputation with a man, did it?

Of course, he doesn't yet realize what a huge favor I'm doing him. This is the equivalent of advance publicity for his new restaurant, which I know will be fabulous.

This is his dream, and you know me. I am all about people realizing their dreams. I'm just not as specific-goal oriented as some.

Speaking of goals, my trek down the Yellow Brick Road got me to thinking. As that story points out, a journey can be a path for learning a lesson or discovering something about yourself. So I'm wondering what my lesson for this journey will be. That falling asleep sitting in a car gives you a stiff neck? That the distance between rest stops is farther apart than the size of the last soda you drank? That uptight guys can be really sexy?

Oops. Strike that last. Too much information and all that. More later...

8

CRAIG FIGURED he would ever after think fondly of Ottawa, Kansas, if only because the motel he and Marlee stayed at featured not only a king-size bed, but a bathtub big enough for two.

And to think before now he'd always judged accommodations by the size of the television and the hours the restaurant stayed open. Amazing how traveling with a woman gave you a whole new perspective.

He glanced at the woman in question, who was battling a wrinkled road map, turning it this way and that and vainly trying to smooth out creases. "What are you doing with that map?" he asked. "Don't you trust me to get us where we're going?"

"I wanted to get an idea of where we are." She blew a stray lock of hair out of her eyes and squinted at the map, tracing her finger along the thin black line of a highway.

"Hello? I thought you had no sense of direction."

"I don't. But I can read a map. We're on U.S. 56, right?"

"You get an A."

She nodded, continuing to drag her finger across the map. "It looks to me like we'll be going right through Farmington, New Mexico."

"You get another A. We'll probably spend the night somewhere near there."

She looked up at him, a gleam in her eyes he'd learn to be wary of. "That's perfect."

"What's perfect?" He forced himself to focus on the road, but every nerve was aware of her as she leaned toward him.

"Didn't you say your parents are in Farmington?"

"Near there." He braced himself for what he was sure was coming. "Why?"

"So we should stop and say hello. We could even spend the night with them."

He shook his head. "We've already discussed this. No."

"Why not? I'm sure they'd love to see you. And I'd love to meet them."

She probably would. She'd waltz right in and charm them both and for the rest of their lives, every time he called his mother would ask about "that darling girl" he'd brought to meet them. "It would be...awkward," he said. "I mean, if I brought a woman with me."

"You mean they wouldn't approve." She sat back. "If it will make things easier, we can pretend everything between us is perfectly platonic. In fact, we can tell them the truth—that we're sharing a ride to Susan and Bryan's wedding."

"My parents don't know Susan or Bryan."

"They don't?" She sounded shocked. "But he's your best friend."

"Yes, but I met him after I moved to D.C." He supposed to someone like her, who told everyone everything about her life, it would seem odd that his parents didn't know his closest friends. But that was the way things were in his family. "We're not very close," he added.

"All the more reason you should make the effort to stop by while you're here."

He frowned. "I don't follow your logic."

"If you're not close, then making a special trip out here to see them probably isn't your idea of a great vacation. So you either don't visit and feel guilty, or you visit and resent the fact that you had to."

He slowed the car and risked a glance at her. "How did you know that?"

She shrugged. "I'm crazy about my family, but it's still a struggle to find the time, and the money, to make a trip back home. And pretty much everybody I know fights with the guilt thing."

He nodded. "Yeah." He loved his folks, but they were easier to love at a distance. Even so, he realized they wouldn't be around forever. Once he opened his restaurant, he wouldn't have the free time to travel cross-country to visit family.

"Can we stop by?" she asked. "I really would like to meet them."

One thing he knew by now—his traveling companion's gentleness was deceptive. She was absolutely relentless and would keep after him until she wore him down. Besides, she'd made some good points. And maybe having her along as a buffer would make a visit with his folks easier. "When we stop for lunch, I'll call them."

She clapped her hands. "That's terrific. I can't wait."

Amazing. Why would she be so fired up to meet his folks? "What about your family?" he asked. "You're from a small town. What would they think if you suddenly showed up with a strange man?"

"They'd be surprised, I guess. I've never brought home a man before." She grinned. "I've brought baklava from a little bakery in Georgetown, and once I brought home a Virginia ham, but never a man."

"But after they got over the surprise, would they be okay with it?"

She shifted in her seat. "Well, my dad would like to believe that I'm a twenty-seven-year-old virgin, and if I brought a guy home it might destroy the illusion, so he'd probably make some comment about big-city ways corrupting a small-town girl."

"You're still a small-town girl."

"What's small-town about me?"

"Hey, I didn't say it was a bad thing. You just have some small-town attitudes. It's cute, really."

"Then why does it sound so patronizing when you say it?" She faced him, arms across her chest. "What do you think is a small-town attitude?"

"Oh, like the way you're careful not to hurt people's feelings, like the mayor and his wife back in Downieville. Or your affinity for weird, kitschy restaurants and motels. You don't see much of that inside the Loop."

"Then you're hanging out with the wrong people. There's nothing particularly 'small town' about being considerate of other people and enjoying offbeat attractions. It's better than being bored and jaded."

"No, you are definitely not bored and jaded." Or particularly sophisticated, which was refreshing, really. The sophisticated people he'd known weren't always much fun. He'd laughed more with Marlee than he had in months. He hadn't even realized how much laughter had been missing from his life until he'd met her.

"My parents would like you, though."

The shift in the conversation startled him. "They would?"

"Of course they would. My mom is a huge fan of cooking shows on TV. She'd be in heaven if she thought I'd snagged a man who knew his way around the kitchen. And my dad would approve because you're so serious and responsible."

He laughed. "So they'd *like* the fact that we're opposites."

She grinned. "I'm sure they'd think we'd make the perfect couple."

The idea made him a little short of breath. He focused his attention on the road, and away from any thought of him and Marlee, together on any kind of permanent basis. They were having fun now, but he was smart enough to know that people as different as the two of them could never make a go of it.

CRAIG HAD GROWN very quiet. Brooding, she suspected, about the visit to his folks. She hoped she hadn't made a mistake, insisting they stop by. He'd said he wasn't close to his family, but that wasn't because they were horrible, was it? People did sometimes have horrible families, but most of the time they were, well, families, with the usual assortment of oddball relatives, slightly eccentric behaviors and hereditary quirks that made up any group of people who'd been thrown together by blood and not by choice.

In any case, she was consumed with curiosity now to meet the two people whose union had resulted in the man beside her.

"Is that your phone?"

She started, and realized that "Girls Just Wanna Have Fun" was drifting up from her totebag. She fished out the phone and checked the caller ID. "Hello, Susan," she said.

"I read your blog."

Of course she had. Marlee sighed. "Is that why you're calling?"

"You're getting awfully philosophical, aren't you? All this stuff about journeys teaching lessons and all that?"

"I happen to believe it's true."

"So are you learning interesting things about the 'Magic Chef'?"

Marlee glanced at her traveling companion. He was frowning, a deep V etched on his forehead as he stared out the windshield. "We're stopping off to say hello to Craig's parents this afternoon."

"He's taking you to meet his parents?" Susan's voice rose in alarm. "Is it that serious between you two?"

The words made her heart do a little tap dance. Were things serious between her and Craig? Sure, she really liked him, and he seemed to like her, but that was a long way from serious, wasn't it? "Don't be silly!" She faked a smile. "We're practically going right through Farmington, so I suggested we stop and say hello. No big deal."

"Right. So what's this about naming his restaurant? Did he ask you to do that?"

"No. I just thought it would be fun."

"Obviously, I've completely misjudged Craig. He never struck me as the fun type."

"You obviously don't know him well."

"And you obviously know him *very* well." Susan laughed. "I can see I'm going to have to revise my opinion of him. Though I'm still not convinced he's the right man for you."

"You don't have to worry."

"Good. Because I told Marcus about you and he's looking forward to meeting you."

"Marcus? Who's that?"

"The groomsman I told you about. Remember? He's perfect for you."

"Oh, yeah." Too bad her idea of "perfect" and Susan's didn't always mesh. She cleared her throat. "You know, it's really nice of you to think of me, but you don't have to go to all that trouble."

"It's no trouble. After all, you're both in the wedding party. You'll have time to hang out and get to know each other."

"Speaking of the wedding, how are things going?" Anything to get Susan out of matchmaking mode.

The ploy worked. Susan groaned. "Crazy! One of my bridesmaids is pregnant and can't fit into her dress, so now it has to be altered and who knows how long that will take? The other one has decided the green satin makes her skin look sallow."

"Tell her nobody will be looking at her anyway. Everyone will be focused on you. Don't let all these little things bother you. Everything will work out. It always does, you know."

"You're right. Thanks. I forget sometimes that you do have a practical side."

"Yeah, that's me. Polly Practical."

Craig shot her a puzzled look. She winked at him.

"Hey, I thought of a name for Craig's restaurant."

"What's that?"

"The Compass. Because he always knows where he's going."

"Very exciting. I'll add it to my list."

"How long is your list so far?"

"You're the first one on it."

"Then I ought to get a special prize."

"Your prize is you have me for a friend. I'd better go now."

"Bye. Can't wait to see you."

"Me, too." She clicked off and stuffed the phone back in her bag.

Craig glanced at her. "Her prize is she has you for a friend?"

"That's pretty special, don't you think?"

He looked back at the road and nodded. "Yeah, I guess it is at that."

She couldn't imagine why his words suddenly made her feel lighter than air but then, her emotions were all over the place lately. Must be hormones. Those little devils always caused trouble.

She glanced at Craig again and the fluttery feeling returned. Not that trouble was such a bad thing....

THEY STOPPED for lunch at a taco stand outside of Clayton, New Mexico, and Craig called his folks from the parking lot. He stood outside the car, a hot wind whipping around him, and tried to plan what he'd say. His mother answered on the fourth ring. "Hello?"

"Mom! It's me, Craig."

"Craig! How are you?"

"I'm fine, Mom. Doing great."

"Are you sure?" She sounded worried. "It's the middle of the day. Shouldn't you be working?"

"He didn't lose his job, did he?" This from his dad, who was apparently standing at his mom's shoulder. "What happened?" he barked.

"Nothing happened. Everything's fine." He took a deep breath, suppressing annoyance. "I took a few days off to drive to a friend's wedding. In fact, I'm in Clayton right now, thought I'd drive down to visit for a bit."

"We'd *love* to see you!" The joy in his mother's voice made him feel guilty all over again for staying away so long.

"If he's in the area, of course we expect him to stop by," his father said.

Of course.

"You can spend the night," Mom said.

He glanced at Marlee, who stood on the other side of the car, smiling at him encouragingly. "I've, ah, got a friend traveling with me."

"That's fine. We can make up the trundle bed in your room if one of you doesn't mind sleeping that close to the floor."

He rolled his eyes. "Mom, I'm not twelve years old, bringing a friend for a sleep-over." Though with Marlee, the thought was appealing—anywhere but at his parent's house. "And this isn't a male friend. It's a woman. She's the maid of honor in the wedding and needed a ride, so—"

"Did you hear that, Ed? He's bringing home a woman!"

"He is? Well I suppose that's better than him bringing home a man."

He grimaced. "We'll see you in a few hours."

He hung up and joined Marlee at the door of the restaurant. "What did they say? Are they excited to see you?"

"Mom sounded excited." He held the door for her. "My dad said he *expected* me to visit since I was this close."

"What did I tell you? If you'd kept to your plan not to stop and they'd found out later, they would have been terribly hurt."

Right. And his dad would have had something else to lecture him about. He sighed. "Come on. Let's get this over with."

"You don't sound exactly thrilled."

"You haven't met my folks yet. Mom's great, but my dad can be hard to take sometimes."

"You only say that because he's your father. I'm

sure he's very charming." She looked over her shoulder at him, a sweet, joyful smile directed his way that made his heart stop for a minute. "He's probably exactly like you."

He couldn't decide if she was teasing him, or completely serious. Before he could ask, she'd scooted ahead of him into a turquoise vinyl booth and was studying the paper menu. "This says their bean burritos are a regional specialty," she said. "Guess I'd better pass on those. Wouldn't want to risk making a bad impression on your folks."

He stared at her, feeling his whole world slip a little on his axis. She was adorable. Absolutely sexy and wonderful. He could hardly believe he felt this way. And about a woman who made fart jokes.

THE BRINKMAN HOME was a nondescript suburban ranch house that looked so much like the houses in the neighborhood Marlee had grown up in that she might have thought she'd been transported back to her home town. Except that Craig's parents had cactus in their front yard instead of pine trees.

They pulled into the paved driveway and the front door opened before they were even out of the car. A trim woman with a bouffant cloud of frosted hair rushed down the steps, followed by a stocky man with a bushy moustache and close-cropped gray curls. The woman stood on tiptoe to hug Craig. "This is such a nice surprise."

Craig returned the embrace, then nodded to Marlee. "Mom, Dad, this is Marlee Jones."

"Marlee, so nice to meet you." Mrs. Brinkman's handshake was warm.

"Hello, Ms. Jones." Mr. Brinkman's voice was gravelly as he solemnly shook her hand.

"Oh please, call me Marlee."

He nodded, still solemn. "All right, Marlee. Come inside, both of you, before we all melt in this heat."

The living room was dark and cool, with a sofa and chair upholstered in plaid polyester and a wall hanging behind the sofa that proclaimed *Semper Fi.* She looked again at Mr. Brinkman's close-cropped hair and erect posture. Of course. He was an ex-marine. Or maybe just a marine. She'd heard one never really got away from the Corps.

She sat on the edge of the sofa and Craig sat beside her. Craig's mom brought them iced tea. "It's a long trip from Washington, isn't it?" she said, settling into a chair across from them. "We made the drive once right after Craig moved there and I told Ed, never again. From now on, we'll fly."

Marlee wrapped both hands around the sweaty tea glass. "I don't really like to fly."

"Oh, well, it doesn't bother me a bit. Now sitting in a car for hours at a time, that's awful on my back. My sciatica—"

"So how is it you know Craig?" Mr. Brinkman interrupted his wife's complaints about her back.

Marlee glanced at Craig, who sat very upright, his arms crossed over his chest. "Dad, don't interrogate her. She just got here."

"I was merely making conversation." Mr. Brinkman turned to her. "You don't mind, do you?"

"Of course not." She turned up the wattage on her smile. Obviously, Craig expected the worst out of his dad, but really, he was pretty typical of most of the dads she knew—interested in what was going on with their grown children, but not adept at subtlety. "My best friend, Susan, is marrying Craig's best friend, Bryan."

"And they introduced you to each other?" Mrs. Brinkman leaned toward them, eyes bright.

Craig coughed. "That's right," he said. "Bryan and Susan got us together."

"So how long have you been dating?" Mr. Brinkman resumed his questioning.

"Oh. Well, we—"

"We're not dating," Craig said. "We're just friends. We agreed to share expenses for the drive out here."

Mrs. Brinkman looked disappointed. Marlee sympathized. She was pretty let down herself. Of course, she'd agreed to the whole "just friends" story, but she wondered if that was how Craig *really* felt. Sure, they'd known each other only a few days, but in that time they'd spent more hours together than she had with her last few relationships, even the ones that had spanned several weeks.

And despite the crazy odds, considering how different the two of them were, she'd grown to really care about her "Magic Chef."

"What kind of work do you do in D.C.?"

Mr. Brinkman's question interrupted her daydreaming. She set her tea glass on a coaster on the coffee table. "I'm an advertising copywriter."

"Advertising!" He nodded. "That's quite a lucrative field, isn't it? If you don't think it's crass of me to ask."

Even if I did, I wouldn't tell you. She kept her smile fixed in place. "It's not very lucrative in the area I work in. I design ad campaigns for nonprofit groups."

"Well, you're young. I'm sure it's a smart move to get that kind of credit on your résumé before you move up the ladder."

"Actually, I prefer—"

Craig leaned forward, his voice sounding weary. "We've had a long drive. Maybe Marlee would like to freshen up before supper."

Okay. So maybe it wasn't a good idea to share her philosophy of job satisfaction versus money with Mr. Brinkman. "Yes." She stood, grateful for the reprieve. "If you could show me to your bathroom?"

"The powder room is this way, dear." Mrs. Brinkman led the way down a short hallway. "And your room is the one at the end there."

"Thank you."

When she came out of the bathroom, Craig was leaning against the wall and watching the bathroom door like a prison guard. He straightened and took her arm. "I'm sorry about my dad. He can come off as brusque."

"Oh, he may be a little gruff, but inside I can see he's a real pussycat."

His frown deepened. "You can?"

"Of course I can. I may not have a sense of direction, but I have a very good sense of what people are really like. And your parents are very nice."

He pulled her toward the bedroom, his voice low. "If you'd rather, we can find a hotel to stay at. Or I could loan you the car and you could go to a hotel."

"Would you chill? You're making way more of this than you need to. They're just being parents, that's all."

He blinked. "Don't tell me your parents give visitors the third degree like that."

"Not exactly, but they'd find some way to learn the same information. Your dad is a little more direct. Which isn't necessarily a bad thing."

His expression remained grim. "It's rude."

She squeezed his arm, wishing she could convince

him to lighten up. "It's all right. And now we have all the preliminaries over with. We can relax and have a nice visit."

He shook his head. "If we do, it will be the first in a long time."

She wanted to ask him about that cryptic remark, but Mrs. Brinkman called them to supper.

The meal itself was very nice—a pot roast with vegetables and a green salad. Sitting around the round wooden table, eating off blue-and-white Corelle plates, she had an eerie sense of déjà vu. How many similar dinners had she sat through with her own family? They'd been nice at the time. The only problem with reliving them now was that no matter how old you were, you never really got away from the roles you'd always played. Waiting for someone to pass the gravy, she couldn't help but feel like the family "baby." Any minute now she expected Mr. Brinkman to offer unsolicited advice on how she should live her life or Mrs. Brinkman to tell her to eat all her peas because young people today didn't get nearly enough vegetables in their diet.

"Have some more peas." Mrs. Brinkman passed the bowl.

"Oh. Thank you." Thankfully, Marlee noted that there were no comments about nutrition. "Everything is so delicious."

"The pot roast is a recipe Craig sent me."

Marlee glanced at Craig, who was hunched over, staring at his plate, for all the world like a sulky teen who didn't want to be drawn into conversation. "Then no wonder it's so good," Marlee said.

"I guess you're still cooking for the politicians up in D.C." Mr. Brinkman speared a carrot.

Craig looked up from his plate and shifted in his

chair across the table from his father. "Yes, I'm still in charge of the Senate Dining Room."

"Everyone knows how good the food is at the dining room," Marlee said. "I'm sure when Craig opens his own restaurant people will stand in line to eat there."

Too late she caught the warning look and shake of Craig's head. Apparently this was something else his parents didn't know about.

"Still talking about that crazy idea?" Mr. Brinkman said.

Craig's face remained impassive. "I've always said I wanted my own restaurant."

"Do you know how many eating establishments fail in this country every year?" Mr. Brinkman brandished his fork like a sword. "And the overhead in a place like D.C. must be ridiculous. It's crazy to take a financial risk like that. Besides, with the economy like it is, people are staying home. They aren't eating out. It's a terrible time to open a restaurant."

Craig sliced his serving of roast into a dozen tiny pieces. "I don't happen to agree with you."

Marlee's stomach hurt. She hated people fighting. And over something so silly. "D.C. isn't like a lot of other cities, Mr. Brinkman," she said. "It's more like New York or Los Angeles, where people eat out all the time." She laughed. "I have friends who have never turned on their ovens. They appreciate when someone like Craig cooks good food for them."

"Hmmph." Mr. Brinkman slathered butter on a roll. "Then let him keep working for someone else. Why risk his own money and reputation just to stroke his ego?"

"You're assuming I'll fail," Craig said. "What if I'm successful?"

"The odds are against it. But when did you ever listen to your old man?"

Honestly, she'd like to take them both in a room and give them a good talking-to. But all she could do at the moment was try to sidetrack the conversation. "Mr. Brinkman, I think you and Mrs. Brinkman should come to D.C. for the grand opening of Craig's restaurant. Then you'll see for yourself what a smart venture it is. Believe me, he won't fail."

They all stared at her. "How do you know that?" Mrs. Brinkman asked.

She swallowed hard. What besides her own intuition and cock-eyed optimism told her Craig would be a success at anything he did? Neither of those reasons was going to be good enough for the Brinkmans. She cleared her throat. "Well, for one thing, I'm going to design a killer advertising campaign for him." She held her head up. "I haven't been associated with a failure yet." She'd also never been in charge of a brand-new commercial campaign, but there was a first time for everything, right?

Craig stared at her, mouth open. In fact, everyone at the table was silent. She congratulated herself on preventing a family feud. "This pot roast really is delicious," she said, focusing on her plate once more. "I'm so glad we decided to stop for a visit."

CRAIG couldn't believe Marlee had come to his defense. Her unrelenting optimism and outsized confidence had saved the meal from becoming yet another battle with his dad—one he'd never win.

After supper his father had retired to the den to read the newspaper. Marlee insisted she and Craig would do the dishes. "So tell me about this fabulous advertising campaign you're designing for a restaurant that doesn't even exist," he said when they were alone in the kitchen.

She blushed. "I just wanted them to see that someone had faith in you."

"I know." He had trouble getting words past the tightness in his chest. "I don't—" He shook his head. "Why would you say something like that?"

She slid a stack of plates into a sink full of dishwater. "Why not? You're obviously not rushing into this restaurant thing. I'm sure you've researched and planned every last detail. And I'm sure you're a wonderful cook."

"How do you know that? You've never eaten my cooking."

She laughed. "All right, but you've been in charge of the Senate Dining Room for how long now?" She began washing and rinsing the plates and stacking them in the drainer.

"Three years." He picked up a towel and began drying the clean dishes.

"So we're talking about powerful men and women who are used to getting what they want. If you didn't deliver, they wouldn't keep you around."

He nodded. "All right. I won't pretend false modesty. I *am* a good cook." Even his dad wouldn't argue that. Despite the tension at the table, the old man had had *two* helpings of the pot roast made from Craig's recipe.

"And you're a good businessman." She dropped a handful of spoons into the silverware basket on the drainer. "At least, you have a degree in business and you're organized and practical."

He nodded.

"So that means you've probably done your homework. You aren't leaping into this blindly."

"Should I be freaked out or flattered that you apparently know me so well?"

She smiled. "I'd go with flattered if I were you."

He laid aside the towel. "So I'm flattered." He slid his hands around her waist, unable to resist touching her. "Now about this advertising campaign?"

"I said that off the top of my head, but I would like to do it, if you'd let me." She glanced over her shoulder at him. "Of course, you might rather hire one of the big established firms."

"I doubt they'd be more creative than you are." He pulled her close. "Besides, I might enjoy working personally with you on this." And working together would give them time to know each other better. Who knew where that might lead, once he had the restaurant up and running smoothly?

She nudged him away. "Better watch it. What if one of your parents walks in on us?"

"Yeah, you're right." He picked up the towel again and resumed drying duties.

"Hey, you're the one who insisted we were 'just friends.'"

He nodded. "I did that for you. You made such a big deal out of telling the mayor of Downieville that we were married so he wouldn't think we were fooling around. I couldn't very well tell my parents we were married, and I didn't think you'd go for telling them we were fooling around."

She laughed and deposited the last of the dishes in the rack. "Underneath all that practicality, you really are a romantic, aren't you?"

He stiffened. "I don't know what you're talking about." The next thing he knew, she'd accuse him of liking chick flicks and kitschy tourist traps.

She wiped her hands on a dishrag and pushed him toward the door. "Go talk to your father."

He made a face. "Do I have to?"

"Pick a neutral subject. Sports or something."

"Only if you join us and play referee."

Her eyebrows rose. "Are you scared to talk to your own father?"

"Let's just say I want to enjoy this evening and keep everything light. With my dad, it's best to have a buffer. Then we can all say we've had a nice visit."

"All right."

On their way out of the kitchen he slipped his arm around her shoulder and gave her a quick hug. "Thanks. Too bad I can't bring you along on all my visits."

She looked up at him, eyes sparkling. "That could be arranged."

The remark stopped him cold. Of course, she was probably just flirting, but what if she was serious? Whoa. Things were moving too fast here. That was what happened whenever you veered off course. Maybe he should have been more adamant about sticking to his original plan.

HERE WE ARE in the Magic Chef's childhood home, making a quick overnight stop, a slight detour from our original travel plans. I believe I've mentioned how the M.C. feels about detours? The man with a plan freaks out a little at anything that throws him off course. Of course, as I've oft stated here, for me the journey is all about detours and distractions. Those side trips and unexpected situations are where the real adventure begins.

For instance, this particular little deviation from our route has shown me that the M.C. and his father are cut from the same cloth—and a very stubborn, rigid, defiant cloth it is. When they've made up their mind about something—whether it's dad's certainty that his son's restaurant is doomed to fail or the son's certainty that dad wants him to fail—neither one is willing to budge. Which is ridiculous, really. Because if they both didn't really love each other, neither one of them would be so bent out of shape about all of this.

Of course, I'm just an irresponsible, flighty chick, so what do I know?

9

MARLEE LAY in bed in the room next to Craig's. She could hear him on the other side of the wall, moving around. Was he undressing now? She smiled at the thought of him stepping out of his jeans. He had really nice legs. Long and muscular. And the cutest little butt....

She rolled over and punched her pillow, trying to drive out the erotic thoughts. She was a guest in his parents' house, for goodness sake. She should behave herself.

Then again, she'd never been very good at coloring in the lines. She wasn't rude or anything, but she did have a penchant for making up her own rules for living. Once, at a team-building seminar for work, the instructor had asked them to write their personal guidelines for life. Marlee's had read:

1. *Be open to everything and prepared for anything.*
2. *If you haven't done it before, why not give it a try?*
3. *No one ever changed the future by sitting around and worrying about it.*
4. *Don't be afraid to swim against the tide.*
5. *When in doubt, choose the unexpected.*

Hmmm. Which might explain why she wasn't exactly on an elevator ride to the top at work. Companies that had team-building exercises tended to put a lot of stock in doing what was expected.

Following her own rule of doing the unexpected, instead of sleeping alone tonight she should sneak next door and seduce Craig. After all, who knew how many more nights they'd have together? Sure, he was all for playing hide the sausage with her now, but once they were back in D.C. he'd be caught up in all his plans and schedules and agendas. She'd seen it before. Any man who kept track of distance traveled, gas mileage and expenses every day of a vacation wasn't going to throw it all away for a carefree love affair.

She rolled onto her back and sighed. It was too bad, really. When she and Craig weren't arguing over petty differences in style, they got along great.

She heard bedsprings creak on the other side of the wall. Apparently, Craig was restless, too. Was he thinking of her? He'd been awfully…friendly in the kitchen. She smiled, remembering. There was something kind of exciting about the idea of sneaking around behind his parents' back, as if she was a teenager again.

And honestly, what was the worst that could happen? If his parents caught them together, it wasn't as if they really *were* teenagers. It might be a little embarrassing, but she'd survived her share of embarrassing moments so far.

She threw back the covers and sat up and felt her way through the darkness to the door. Anticipation fizzed through her as she slipped into the hall and tiptoed to Craig's room. She eased open the door and scooted inside before anyone could come along and see her.

She stood just inside the door, trying to orient herself to the layout of the room. The power light from the computer monitor on a desk to her left gave off a faint green glow, enough for her to see the bed directly across from her and the silhouette of a figure in it.

"Craig?" she whispered.

"Marlee? What are you doing here?" He sat up and reached toward the bedside lamp.

"No, don't turn on the light." She hurried to the bedside and grabbed the edge of the blanket. "Scoot over and let me in."

He slid over and she joined him under the covers. "What are you doing here?" he asked again.

"I came to see you." She snuggled close. He was naked except for his boxers.

"You shouldn't be here," he said, even as his arm went around her.

"Why not?" She kissed his neck. "This is fun."

"This is crazy." But he kissed her back. "My parents might hear us," he said, his lips against hers.

"Not if we're careful." She wrapped her leg around his waist and snuggled closer. "It's kind of exciting to sneak around like this, don't you think?"

"It is, but…"

She silenced him with another long kiss. "Come on. Show me how excited you are," she whispered.

Craig's mind might object to her little midnight seduction, but his body was definitely getting into the spirit of things. "You really are incorrigible," he said as he slipped his hand beneath her nightshirt.

"Is anyone ever corrigible?" She nipped at his ear. "It doesn't sound very pleasant, does it? Incorrigible is much more fun."

"Do you ever take things seriously?" He had her nightshirt off now, and was kissing his way down to her breasts.

"You want me to be…serious?" He was doing amazing things with his mouth. "Oh, yes. That's wonderful."

He moved lower, his hand tugging at her underwear. "You're right. I can't imagine you being serious."

"I'm seriously enjoying making love with you."

"Ah, well that's a start, isn't it?" He succeeded in divesting her of her underwear and slid lower still in the bed. "After all, this is serious business."

After that, neither of them said much for quite a while, though she had to bite down on her knuckles to keep from crying out as he worked his wonderful magic on her. And to think he'd tried to talk her out of this!

Later, she lay in his arms, eyes closed, smiling. Was there anything more comfortable than lying in a man's arms after you'd just made love? Anything more satisfying and relaxing…

"Marlee! Wake up!" Craig's whisper was urgent. He shook her gently and she opened her eyes, surprised to see light leaking around the edges of the room's curtains.

"Wh-what time is it?" She struggled into a sitting position.

"Shhh. It's after seven. You've got to hide."

"Craig?" Mrs. Brinkman tapped on the door. "It's almost seven-thirty. You told me you wanted to get an early start this morning."

"Thanks, Mom. I'll be right up." He gave Marlee a desperate look.

She slid out of bed, gathering her clothes from the floor. She could hide in the bathroom, then exit the door on the other side and head for her room….

The bedroom door creaked open. "What would you like for breakfast?"

Moving faster than she would have thought possible at this early hour, Marlee dove under the bed, her feet disappearing from view as Craig's mom stopped by his bedside. She held her breath, listening. It would be bad enough trying to explain what she was doing in Craig's bed. (Though considering they were both naked, the answer would be pretty obvious.) It would be beyond mortifying to try to come up with a plausible reason why she was cowering—still naked—under the bed.

"Mom! You can't barge in here without knocking." The bed creaked and she imagined Craig sitting up, the covers pulled around him.

"As if I don't know what you look like naked. Or do you think I closed my eyes every time I changed a diaper?"

Marlee stifled a giggle. Craig was no doubt blushing red as a beet by now.

"Have you seen Marlee?" Mrs. Brinkman asked.

"No! Why would I have seen Marlee?"

"She's not in her room. I stopped by to ask what she'd like for breakfast and she wasn't there."

"Maybe she's taking a shower."

"No, she's not in the bathroom, either."

"Maybe she went jogging or something."

"By herself? I hope she didn't get lost. The street signs around here can be confusing."

"I'm sure she'll be all right, Mom."

"She seems like a very nice girl."

"Yes, she is. Now could I have some privacy to get dressed, please?"

"Are you all right?" Mrs. Brinkman moved closer to the bed. The tips of her sandals were only inches from Marlee's nose. She wore bright pink polish on her toenails.

"Yes, I'm all right. Why wouldn't I be all right?"

"You're very irritable. When you were a boy I could always tell when you were coming down with something because you'd be so grouchy."

"I'm fine, Mom. Now please would you leave me alone?"

"All right. I'll go make breakfast. Is French toast all right?"

"French toast is great."

Mrs. Brinkman's toes disappeared from view. Marlee waited a few minutes after she heard the door shut, then wiggled out from under the bed and dusted herself off.

Craig threw back the covers and reached for his pants. "This is crazy," he whispered. "Why did I ever let you talk me into this?"

She stepped into her panties, then reached for her nightshirt. "You didn't exactly fight me off last night, you know."

"You were in my bed. Practically naked. No man would be able to think straight under those circumstances."

Was that a compliment? Except, what kind of compliment was it when the man who said the words was scowling at you? "You're making a big deal out of nothing," she said.

"It's not nothing. My mom almost walked in on us just now. What you did was completely irresponsible."

"What *I* did? Excuse me, but that was not a one-woman show last night." She put her hands on her hips and glared at him. Arguing without raising your voice was frustrating. The most they could do was scowl and hiss at each other like a pair of cobras.

He had the grace to flush. "You're right. But we agreed that while we were here, in my parents' house, we would keep things platonic."

"Oh, lighten up. So what if they found out we had sex? What's the worst that could happen?"

"The worst that could happen is that they'd know I lied to them. And they'd wonder what else I lied about."

Ugh. She hated the nasty feeling that crept over her—a combination of guilt and accompanying self-loathing. She took a deep breath and nodded. "I see your point. I'm sorry. But it's okay. Nothing happened."

"What happened is that I let you talk me into doing something I never would have done otherwise."

"What's wrong with that? You need to loosen up."

"No, I don't." His voice rose.

"Shhhh." She grabbed his hand and dragged him into the bathroom. She shut the door behind them and turned on the shower. Now they could talk without being overheard. She faced him. "What has gotten into you?"

"What do you mean?" He avoided looking at her.

"Why am I the enemy all of a sudden? And why do I get the feeling that this really doesn't have that much to do with your parents?"

He looked at the floor, then at the ceiling, fists clenched at his sides. Finally he lowered his gaze to meet hers. "I read your blog."

"You did? When?"

"Last night. I saw the computer in there and thought I'd check my e-mail. Then I decided to see what that Web site of yours was about."

It pleased her to know he was that interested. "Then what's the problem?"

His expression remained grim, but he said nothing.

She nodded. "I see. You didn't like something I wrote."

"You said I was 'stubborn, rigid and defiant.'"

She winced. "I didn't mean that as a bad thing, exactly."

"Is that how you see me—some uptight idiot you need to make over?"

"Craig, that's not what I meant." She reached for him, but he stepped back.

"You know, there's nothing wrong with being responsible and acting like an adult. Maybe you should try it sometime."

"Oh, that's rich, coming from you!" Rage momentarily fogged her vision and she had to restrain herself from slapping him.

"What do you mean by that?"

"You didn't like what I wrote, but instead of saying anything to me last night, you went ahead and slept with me. Is that being 'responsible' and 'adult'?"

His face reddened, though from anger or shame she couldn't tell. "I told you I wasn't thinking straight."

"So don't blame your mixed-up head on me."

"I'd better go." He turned and left the bathroom.

She stared after him, wishing she had the nerve to go after him and settle this. But guilt over her own role in the evening held her back. After a minute, she stripped off her clothes and stepped into the shower.

When she'd written those things about him in her blog, she'd never expected him to read them. The last thing she'd wanted was to hurt his feelings, but obviously she had. What had she been thinking?

It was like he said—she obviously *hadn't* thought. The impulsiveness she usually took such pride in had come back to bite her in the butt. But that remark about her not behaving like an adult was a really low blow. After all, that wasn't some *child* he'd slept with, was it?

She stepped out of the shower and began drying her hair. After wiping the fog from the mirror over the sink, she took a critical look at herself. So much for the happy-go-lucky free spirit. Her impulsiveness had hurt someone she really cared about, not to mention almost embarrassing him in front of his parents.

So much for having a wonderful fantasy trip away from her real life. Right now, it sucked to be her.

BY THE TIME Marlee arrived at the breakfast table, the ends of her hair still damp and her skin glowing from her shower, Craig had worked up a healthy case of remorse. She was right—he'd overreacted this morning. After all, he had been a willing participant in their lovemaking, and to tell the truth, he'd fantasized about sneaking over to *her* bedroom before she'd shown up in *his* room.

The difference between the two of them was that while he'd tortured himself with fantasies of slipping into her bed and making illicit love to her, she'd gotten out of her bed and made things happen.

She'd said as much in her blog, hadn't she? He was the kind of man who "freaks out a little at anything that throws him off course." Though the words had stung, he'd recognized the truth in them. And he knew Marlee well enough to know there was no malice behind them. He grimaced, remembering how he'd lectured her on being immature and irresponsible while he'd acted like a spoiled little boy who couldn't take criticism.

Somehow, he managed to fake it through breakfast, then he and Marlee loaded the car and were on their way. They were scarcely out of the driveway when she turned to him. "I'm sorry about the blog. I'll take the entries about you down."

"No. You have a right to your opinion." God, he sounded so stiff. He glanced at her. "I mean, I may have overreacted."

"No, you're right. You're certainly entitled to your privacy."

"I doubt if too many people would ever figure out I was the 'Magic Chef.'" He didn't feel very magical right now.

"I'm sorry about what happened last night, too," she said.

"You are?" This made him feel even more bleak.

"I mean, I'm not sorry it happened." She looked down and smoothed hands along her thighs. "But I shouldn't have risked it. I didn't think about the consequences if we were caught. Like you said—it was irresponsible."

She was admitting guilt, so why did *he* feel so bad? "Look, let's forget about it," he said. "We survived the visit and we only have two more days until we're in San Diego."

She sat up straighter. "You're right. But I'm going to try to do better from now on. If you can learn to be more spontaneous from me, then I can certainly learn to be more responsible from you."

"Sounds like a deal." He smiled at her. He had his doubts about her suddenly becoming a poster child for responsibility and organization, but who cared? There were worse things in the world than being spontaneous and joyful. If he hung around with her long enough, he might even learn to embrace her love of detours and side trips.

Or maybe he'd love embracing her and learn to live with the rest.

ARGUMENT with M.C. today. One of those that leave you wishing you could hit the rewind button. Or turn your life into a movie set and call "Take two, please."

He accused me of being—get ready for it—irresponsible and immature.

My devoted fans, is that how you see me? I always thought of myself as the "different drummer" type. I mean, it's not my fault I lost my driver's license, is it? And what's wrong with living life on my own terms?

Still, I have to admit I do often act without thinking about the consequences, and I can see the irresponsibility in that. And I'm certainly mature enough to admit when I'm wrong.

(And Susan, if you're reading this, don't bother to call, because I'm turning my phone off. I'm not in the mood to talk right now.)

I'm trying to do better. To show him—and myself—that I can be a mature, responsible adult. No matter how boring that is. Today, when we passed all the signs advising us to See Rock City, I didn't suggest we stop, though I know it would have been a kick if we did.

And when M.C. pulled up at your standard Econo Inn for the night, I refrained from pointing out that we'd passed the Tipi Lodges on the way into town. (They were absolutely adorable—each little cottage constructed to resemble a real tipi.)

So far, all this conventionality has been dreadfully dull. I don't know how much longer I can keep it up.

CRAIG KNEW something was up when they drove past two dozen See Rock City signs and Marlee never said a word. After they passed the sixth sign in an hour he glanced over at her and saw that she was actually biting her lip. He felt like he'd swallowed lead. "Is something wrong?" he asked.

"No. Why would you think something is wrong?" She stared out the front windshield. "When do you think we'll reach San Diego?"

"Tomorrow afternoon. In time for dinner, anyway."

She nodded. "That's good."

And that was it. No speculation on what they should have for dinner or attempts to persuade him to make a side trip to explore Rock City which was, after all, the King of Kitsch when it came to tourist attractions. Exactly the kind of thing he detested and she adored.

So he ought to be happy they were bypassing it without protest from her. Instead, he felt guilty. On the one hand, it was great to be on schedule for a change, the miles winding out behind them, everything going smoothly. On the other hand, this serious, solemn version of Marlee worried him. She didn't act angry with him, exactly. When she spoke to him she was pleasant, and even smiled occasionally. But she didn't suggest any games of Truth or Dare, or sing along with the radio, or pepper him with questions about his plans for his restaurant.

True, all of these things had annoyed him at the beginning of the trip, but now he found he missed them. The hours passed too slowly with only silence between them, and the scenery was stupifyingly dull without her amusing take on it.

In late afternoon they reached their destination for the evening, Lake Havasu City, Arizona. On the outskirts of town, a faded sign beckoned: Tipi Lodges. Craig stared at the cluster of tourist cabins, each topped by a conical roof resembling a Native American tipi, each one painted a different crayon color, faded by the sun to pastel shades of peach, tur-

quoise and pink. Marlee sat up straighter and leaned
forward to stare.

He waited for her to suggest they stop, and was
even prepared to give in, but she remained silent. He
felt sad as he turned into the Econo Inn parking lot.

Dinner was likewise a solemn affair. Afterward
they watched TV and took turns in the bathroom.
When he emerged from the bathroom after changing
out of his clothes, she was in bed with the lights out,
her back to him.

He slipped in beside her and pulled the covers up
over his shoulder. She didn't move, though he was sure
she wasn't asleep. Not exactly the way he'd planned on
spending the last night of this road trip, but no surprise
considering the distance between them all day.

He closed his eyes and tried to get comfortable.
Yes, this new "serious" version of Marlee definitely
wasn't the one he preferred.

MARLEE wished now that she'd insisted on separate
rooms for the night. Lying here, only inches away
from Craig, not touching him, was too hard.

But touching him would be even worse. This was
their last night together. No matter how wonderful
making love with him was, everything tonight
would be tainted by the knowledge that they'd soon
be going their separate ways.

She couldn't bear it. Sure, maybe she'd started out
telling herself she could approach this as a fun fling,
but her heart had made her a liar. She *did* want more
from Craig. Knowing she couldn't have it hurt worse
than anything she'd ever experienced.

Susan was right. She'd been crazy to get involved
with Craig Brinkman.

But she wasn't crazy enough to keep adding to the

hurt. So no more lovemaking. No more touching or kissing or hugging.

She squeezed her eyes more tightly shut and felt hot tears slide down her cheeks. She could be strong. She could do this. After all, she was mature and responsible.

And miserable. Don't forget miserable. Honestly, was anything that made you feel so bad really worth the effort?

As she drifted off to sleep, Craig's warmth at her back, a drowsy voice inside her head answered: *Probably not.*

THE NEXT MORNING, half an hour down the road from the motel, Marlee took off her pink rhinestone sunglasses and turned to Craig. "I'm sorry," she said. "I really tried being practical and responsible and all that, but it's so damn *boring!*"

Relief flooded him. *Here* was the Marlee he knew. "I never said you needed to be those things." He flushed, remembering the argument they'd had at his parents. "Or if I did, I didn't mean you couldn't have fun, too."

"Well, I *am* ready to have fun." She lowered the sunglasses into place once more and picked up the map. "What's on schedule for today?"

"A lot of empty desert, as far as I can tell. We should be in San Diego by this evening."

San Diego and then what? What would happen to their relationship when they were no longer spending twenty-four hours a day in each other's company? He'd never met anyone more unlike himself, and yet most of the time he felt more comfortable with her than he had with anyone else. Ever. So what did that mean? And was now really the time to find that out, considering all the other decisions he had to make about his life and his career and his future?

Why did life have to be so complicated and messy? Maybe that was one of the reasons he enjoyed cooking so much. You put ingredients together in a recipe and they almost always came out the way they were supposed to. But no one had a foolproof recipe for living.

Marlee slipped a CD into the stereo and Lyle Lovett sang a Texas swing number. She snapped her fingers and swayed in time to the beat. "Welcome back," he said.

She stopped moving and stared at him. "I haven't been gone, silly."

"Yes, you have. All of yesterday my passenger was some imposter who looked like you but was far too serious."

She looked at him warily. "Do you still think I'm irresponsible and immature?"

"I think you're you. Marlee. And that's all you have to be." *All I want you to be.* But he didn't say the last words out loud. It was too soon for that kind of confession, not when the future was so uncertain.

"Oh look!" She pointed ahead to a sign by the side of the road. Desert and Museum were the only words he made out before they sped past.

"We should stop," she said, turning to him.

He opened his mouth to say no. After all, a stop would put them behind. But really, what difference would a couple of hours make? "All right. I guess we could use a break."

Her smile competed with the sun for warming up the interior of the car. He grinned back at her, feeling as if he'd done something heroic, instead of agreeing to visit some dinky desert museum.

"The sign said to take the next right," she said.

"Then what?" He put on his blinker, though there wasn't another car in sight.

"Then we watch for more signs."

They turned onto a narrow paved road which became a dirt lane after only a few miles. "This museum must not get a lot of traffic," he said.

"I guess not." She peered out the front window, looking for signs. "I hope we didn't miss another turnoff."

"I haven't seen any other roads," he said. "Maybe we should go back and check the sign again."

"No, it'll be okay," she said. "We'll drive a little farther."

They passed a gray wooden house surrounded by a sagging fence. "We could stop and ask someone," he said, slowing in front of the house.

"No, it's okay. Let's just drive. If we don't find it soon, we can turn around." She smiled. "After all, some of my best adventures have come from seeing where things lead when I get lost."

"We're not lost." After all, the road led back to the main highway, though that was some miles away by now.

He drove on, but now there was nothing around them but desert. No signs. No houses. Not even fences. They bumped over the rutted road, dust boiling up behind them. He had a bad feeling about this. "I'm turning around," he said.

She sank back in the seat. "I guess you're right. The sign did look kind of old. Maybe the museum closed down."

He shifted into Reverse and prepared to do a Y turn in the middle of the deserted road. With an awful *clunk!* the car refused to move. The engine coughed a few times, then died.

Silence wrapped around them like a layer of cotton. He could feel Marlee's eyes on him as he stared out the windshield. His knuckles began to ache and he pried his hands from the steering wheel and turned the key. The car made a humming, high-pitched noise and refused to start.

"What's wrong?" Marlee asked in a small voice.

"I don't know." He reached down for the hood release, then got out and walked around to the front of the car. The desert heat hit him like a furnace, and he squinted against the glare in spite of his sunglasses. He heard the passenger door slam shut as Marlee followed him.

The engine compartment was a puzzle of rubber and metal, but after a moment of staring into it, he located the problem. He reached down and fished out a long strip of rubber. "Busted belt." He handed it to Marlee, then reached for his phone. God knows how long it would take Triple A to reach a place like this.

His heart and his head pounded as he listened to the phone. He flipped it shut and stuck it back in his pocket. "No signal," he said grimly.

"Let me try mine." She leaned in the car and pulled her phone from her bag. Her expression grew bleak as she looked at the screen. "I don't have any service either." She stared at the broken belt in his hand. "What do we do now?"

He looked around at the empty landscape around them. Not another house for miles, and they were the only car they'd seen for the last hour or more. He tilted his head up and squinted at the cloudless sky and relentless sun. "I think we're in real trouble now," he said.

10

MARLEE STARED at the confusing jumble of parts and plastic that made up the car's engine and tried to think of something helpful to say. Something practical and responsible.

But she wasn't any of those things, was she? If she was helpful, practical and responsible, they wouldn't be standing here right now, without so much as a shade tree in sight, much less a garage or another person who could help them. A practical, responsible person never would have suggested setting out across the desert in search of a museum that apparently didn't even exist. "Maybe we could make a belt—something temporary to hold until we got to a garage, or at least to where we have phone service."

He leaned over and stared down into the engine. "Maybe. Do you have any panty hose or a scarf or something that would be long enough?"

"No. I don't usually wear scarves or panty hose, though I'd planned to buy hose in San Diego to wear to the wedding. Maybe we could rip up a dress or something." She'd gladly sacrifice one of her thrift-store finds for a way out of here.

He shook his head. "Thanks, but even if we did that, I don't think I could make it work. I don't have any tools or anything." He slammed the hood shut. "After all, I'm a chef, not a mechanic."

She squinted toward the horizon, hoping against hope to see an approaching car, or some sign of life. The flat, almost barren ground shimmered in the heat, the emptiest place she'd ever seen. They could film a moon shot out here, no problem. "Where are those ruby slippers when you need them?" she asked.

He opened the car door and took out the two bottles of water they'd purchased that morning and handed one to her. "Come on, Dorothy. We'd better start walking."

"Where to?" She took the water bottle and walked around to the passenger side to retrieve her tote bag. Most of her emergency supplies were gone, but she still had a candy bar and some sunscreen.

"Back to that house. Maybe they've got a phone we can use to call a garage."

She set the tote on the hood of the car and took out the tube of sunscreen and began rubbing the lotion on her arms. She could already feel the back of her neck burning. They'd passed that house a long time ago, hadn't they? "How far do you think it is to that house?" she asked.

He stared down the road. "I don't know. Five miles? Maybe more."

She swallowed hard. "That far?"

"Maybe farther. Do you have a better idea?"

She ducked her head. "No." Her bright idea to see the museum had gotten them here in the first place. "You'd better put some of this on." She passed him the tube of sunscreen. "Your face is already red."

"My face is red because it's over one hundred degrees out here." But he slathered some of the lotion across his nose and cheeks and returned the tube.

She stuffed the tube back in the tote bag and searched through the contents, hoping in vain to find something that would help them. A fashion magazine. Two tubes of lipstick. A package of Band-Aids. A pen. Three condoms. Right. Fat chance of using those out here.

"Come on," Craig said. "Let's go."

The shoulder of the road was rough and uneven, so they ended up walking down the center of the lane. "I guess not many people travel out this way," she said, kicking aside a fist-size rock.

"Why would they? There's nothing out here but lizards and rocks."

"I guess the museum must have closed."

"Yeah."

He walked ahead of her, head down, hands shoved in his pockets. The sun beat down on them until she felt like the inside of her head was baking. She stopped and took a drink, then discovered that her bottle of water was more than half gone. What would happen when she ran out?

She hurried to catch up with Craig. "I'm sorry I suggested we take that turnoff," she said. "But I couldn't have known something like this would happen."

"No, you couldn't have," he agreed. But he didn't raise his head to look at her, or slow his pace at all.

So much for thinking sharing her guilt would make her feel better. She trudged along, trying to ignore her throbbing head and aching feet. The inside of her mouth felt as though she'd been munching insulation. She allowed herself another sip of water and glanced over her shoulder at the car. It was much smaller now, but she could still see it, so they must not have walked very far. The thought made her queasy. If she felt this bad already, would she even make it to that house?

She faced forward again, focusing on Craig's back.

He had a nice back. Very sexy. She'd always been fond of men's backs, dating to her freshman year of high school, when she'd spent every deadly boring economics class admiring Kevin Karnowski's back. Kevin played football and sat directly in front of her. His wide shoulders effectively blocked her from the view of Ms. Eckols, the teacher, and were the basis of hours of pleasant fantasy.

She raised her water bottle to her lips again and was rewarded with a single warm sip. She stared at the now-empty bottle in horror. She'd meant to ration its contents but had been so busy trying to distract herself she hadn't paid attention to how much she was drinking.

She squinted up at the sky. No sign of a cloud. Chances didn't look good for a sudden rainstorm, either. How long did it take to die of heat stroke? What did it feel like, anyway? How long would it be before someone found her body, and when they did, would it be all shriveled up and desiccated, like a mummy? To think of all the money she'd spent on moisturizers and sunscreen and no one would ever know!

The thought depressed her so much she slowed her steps. Craig stopped and looked back at her. "Are you all right?"

"Sure. I'm fine." She looked up and flashed a big smile, but she had trouble focusing. When did he get so blurry? And why were there suddenly *two* of him?

"Whoa there. Careful." Suddenly, he was by her side, steadying her. "Lean on me. That's it." He brought his water bottle to her lips.

"I can't drink all your water," she said.

"Go ahead. You look like you're about to pass out."

So she drank, probably more than she should, but she couldn't stop herself. He wet a handkerchief with some of the rest of the water and draped it on top of her head. Her vision cleared and she was able to stand up straight. "Thanks," she said. "I feel pretty silly."

"Do you think you can keep walking?"

She looked around. During her brief dizzy spell, nothing had changed. Unlike Dorothy, no Oz awaited her, only more hot, empty desert. "I don't have much choice, do I?"

They walked side by side after that, Craig reaching out a hand to steady her whenever she stumbled over a rock or an uneven spot in the road. So maybe he didn't hate her. Or maybe it was just his strong sense of responsibility kicking in.

"I think I see something up ahead."

She didn't know how long she'd been stumbling along beside him when his words roused her. She raised her head and stared past his pointing finger. At first she didn't see anything new, then gradually she made out a distant roof line. "Is that the house we passed in the car earlier?" she asked.

"I think it is."

She wanted to break into a run, but frankly, didn't have the strength. So she settled for walking a little faster, wondering if the inhabitants of the house would be too shocked if she stripped off her clothes and stood in the shower while Craig phoned the garage. All that cool water would feel so wonderful.

A long time ago the house had probably been painted but these days the walls were the uniform gray of weathered lumber. The metal roof was streaked with orange rust and a very faded, very dusty sofa sat on the front porch, stuffing leaking out of one of its cushions.

The porch itself seemed solid enough, hardly shaking as they walked across it. Craig pounded on the door, the report of his fist on the dried wood echoing in the stillness. Marlee held her breath, listening for footsteps. But the only sound she heard was her own pounding pulse.

He knocked again. When no one answered, she slumped. "I don't think anyone's at home."

He walked over to the window and peered in. "There are a lot of boxes and papers and stuff piled up inside." He shook his head, a worried look on his face. "It doesn't look like anyone's been here in a long time."

She sank to the steps, too shaky to stand any longer. "It feels good to get out of the sun and rest."

He came and stood over her. "We can't stay here," he said.

"I'm too tired to move." She leaned her head against and porch post and closed her eyes. "And thirsty."

She heard his steps move away, but didn't bother to look up. Maybe he planned to leave her here while he went for help. Wasn't that brave of him? Positively heroic.

She didn't know how long she was alone; she thought she might have dozed. She was awakened by a trickle of water down the side of her face, dripping onto her head from somewhere above.

She sat up with a start and looked up into Craig's grinning face. He held a bucket over her head, tipping it just enough to dribble a thin stream of wetness over her. "Where did you get that?" she asked.

"There's a well out back." He set the bucket down and offered her his water bottle. "Drink up."

She drained the whole thing, while he re-wet his

handkerchief and wiped his face. It was amazing how much better the water made her feel. She leaned over and dug in her totebag and found a chocolate bar. "Want half a Snickers?" she asked.

He sat beside her on the steps. "Sounds great."

The candy was half melted and very soft, but she didn't know when she'd tasted anything so delicious. "What should we do now?" she asked as she licked the last of the chocolate from her fingers.

"We should probably go back to the car. If someone finds it, they won't know to look for us here."

"I'm too pooped to walk all that way, at least in this heat."

He nodded. "Then I guess we stay here." He nodded toward the road. "One good thing about a dirt road is that you can see someone coming from a long way off. We can watch and flag down anyone who passes by."

"Sounds like a plan." She stretched her arms over her head. Now that she'd had food and water and was in the shade, death no longer seemed imminent. Life wasn't great, but she could deal.

"Do you think maybe this was the museum and now it's closed?" she asked.

"I think you'd have to be crazy to put a museum way out here." He hunched forward, elbows on his knees, watching the road. "I don't suppose you have any more candy bars in that bag of yours?"

She opened the bag and searched through the contents. "Sorry. I've got gum." She offered him a stick.

He took it. "I wish I'd eaten a bigger breakfast."

"I'd do degrading things for an ice cream cone right now."

"Too bad I don't have any ice cream." He grinned at her.

She laughed and leaned back on her elbows. "If you did you could make us some fantastic dessert, like baked Alaska."

"Charlotte bombe."

"What's that?"

"Ladyfingers lining a round metal mold, covered with a shell of chocolate cream, filled with raspberry ice cream and topped with chocolate sauce and whipped cream."

"You're killing me," she moaned. "That sounds divine." She glanced at him. "How come you don't weigh four hundred pounds, working around food like that all the time?"

He shrugged. "I'm too busy preparing the food to eat it most of the time."

"How did you end up being a chef? I mean, I know *why* you chose that profession, but how did that even come to be a choice?"

He stared off into the distance before answering. In fact, she'd decided he wasn't going to answer when he finally spoke. "When I was in high school, my dad wanted me to play football. But I was totally uninterested and not particularly coordinated. I tried out for the team to please him, but of course I didn't make it."

She frowned, remembering his marine dad. "Was he upset?"

"*Disappointed* is probably a better word. He didn't say much, but then, he and I have never talked all that much." He leaned back against the step behind him. "Anyway, since I couldn't play football, I had to sign up for one more course to have enough credits. The only electives available were art, band, German and something called Family and Consumer Science. I've always liked science, so I signed up." He laughed. "Turns out it was really Home Economics with a new name."

"Oh, my." She put her hand to her mouth. "I'll bet your dad was thrilled with that."

"I don't know what he thought, but I ended up having a great time. I was one of only three guys in the class, so I was surrounded by girls. The focus that semester was on cooking and I found out I really enjoyed messing around in the kitchen, trying out recipes and stuff. Plus, everybody likes to eat, so it's easy to impress people when you can cook."

"And the rest is history."

He nodded. "I got a job in a restaurant and after graduation I got a business degree and then attended the Culinary Institute."

"I'm impressed that you knew what you wanted to be at such a young age." Not surprised, really, but impressed. She'd known from the first day they'd met that here was a guy who had his whole life figured out, while she had trouble thinking as far ahead as next week.

"So how did you decide to go into advertising work?" he asked.

She made a face. "*Decide* isn't exactly the right word. I sort of wandered into the job, really."

He looked at her. "You *wandered* into it?"

"I was supposed to meet a friend downtown for lunch and I accidentally ended up in the wrong suite of offices at her building. This guy at the front desk saw me and asked if I was there to apply for the job. I was looking for a job at the time, so I said yes."

"And they hired you? For a job you knew nothing about?"

"It was a receptionist's job. But I learned a little here and there, and when a copywriter position came open, I was hired." She smiled. "I always thought it was fate, really."

"You really believe in that stuff, don't you?" he asked.

"Yeah. Yeah, I really do." Fate, chance, karma—whatever you wanted to call it, she'd had a lot of good things come into her life that she hadn't expected.

Then, of course, there were things like today. She didn't want to think about how this might end up. She closed her eyes and rested her head against the porch post. The long walk and the stifling heat made her drowsy. Maybe she could fall asleep and when she woke up she'd discover this was all merely a bad dream....

"Marlee! Wake up!"

She opened her eyes and Craig was standing over her. "What is it?" She sat up straighter and looked toward the road. "Is someone coming?"

"No, but I've got an idea." He pointed toward the side of the house. "What do you see?"

She stared in the direction he indicated, but all she saw was part of a sagging barbed wire fence, cactus and a leaning shed. "I don't see anything special. What is it?"

"The wires. Telephone wires. That means this place has a phone."

"Or it did." She stood and brushed herself off. "So what are you going to do about it?"

He walked to the front window and looked in. "I'm going to break in and use the phone to call for help."

She looked around them. The area was still deserted, but a lifetime of being a law-abiding citizen (well, except for those speeding tickets) made her feel guilty at the thought of even innocent burglary. "What if someone shows up while you're breaking in?" she asked.

"No one's going to show up." He tried to shove

up the sash of the front window. "And if they do, I'll explain what happened. It's not like we have anywhere else we can go for help."

"You're right. Do you think you can get in?"

"I'll get in somehow." He picked up a rock that had apparently served as a doorstop at one time or another and studied the window. "Stand back," he warned.

She stepped back to the edge of the porch, and cringed as he heaved the rock through the window. Glass shattered and fell in jagged shards. He picked out some of the bigger pieces, then reached up and turned the lock. With a grunt, he shoved the sash up and climbed inside.

She looked around guiltily, then took a deep breath and ducked in after him.

The inside of the house was dark and dusty, the front room crowded with cardboard boxes and old furniture, like the contents of a junk store that specialized in garage-sale rejects.

She picked her way around a burnt-orange velvet sofa and a green plaid chair and followed Craig into the kitchen. This room was neater, with a circa-1960s dinette set and harvest gold appliances. And an avocado-green princess phone.

She held her breath as Craig picked up the phone, then dialed. She raised her arms in a silent cheer as he explained their situation to the person on the other end of the line.

He scarcely had time to get the receiver back in the cradle when she leaped on him. "We're saved!" She threw her arms around him and kissed his cheek, relief ricocheting through her like steel bearings in a pinball machine.

"Triple A is on the way." He held her close.

"To save the day." Her lips met his. What had begun as a quick celebratory embrace quickly turned passionate. The combination of an adrenaline rush and sheer joy at getting out this mess alive coalesced into an attack of horniness.

Craig felt it too. He ran his hand up under her shirt and his eyes took on a sleepy, sexy look that put her every nerve on alert. "Do you think that table would support both of us?" he asked.

Reluctantly, she shook her head. "I think we'd better not risk it. The way our luck's run lately, either Triple A or the people who own this place would walk in and find us getting down and dirty on their kitchen table."

He looked over her shoulder at the table. "It is tempting."

"Oh, yeah. It's tempting." She looked into his eyes, weak all over again at the thought of what might have happened to them if they hadn't found a working phone. She moved out of his arms and took a deep breath. "You know, I've been thinking."

"About what?"

"About us." She crossed her arms over her chest. "We're almost to San Diego and I guess...I just want you to know that...that it's been fun. But I don't want you to think I expect things to go on like they have been. I mean, once we're not traveling together and all." She swallowed. Damn, she'd thought she could do this. She could be practical and sensible and mature and...and the grim look on his face didn't make things any easier.

"What are you trying to say?" he asked.

She squeezed her arms together even tighter, as if she could hold back the flood of emotion that threatened to overcome the logical arguments she'd been making with herself all day. "I'm only saying that I know you have your restaurant to see to, and that we're two very different people and things would probably never work out with us so I understand if we don't really see each other after this."

He stared at her for a long moment, blinking, his expression unreadable. He didn't look angry, exactly. And he didn't look truly disappointed, either. More... stunned. "Say something," she prompted.

He opened his mouth, closed it again, then cleared his throat. "We are really different, aren't we?"

She nodded.

"And the restaurant is going to take a lot of my time."

"I know that. That's why I said—"

He held up his hand. "I know what you said. I guess I'm a little surprised, that's all."

"Why are you surprised?"

He shook his head. "I've never had a woman be so...so reasonable about things before. Usually when two people break up, there's a big fight, isn't there?"

She straightened her shoulders. "You didn't think I could be reasonable?" In addition to being immature and irresponsible, was she also unreasonable?

"No. No. Obviously you are." He looked around, then his eyes finally met hers again. "It's been fun. And I hope I do see you again. At least as a friend."

She nodded. "Right."

"I guess I'll go look for a piece of cardboard to fix that window," he said after a moment. "We can leave a note for the owners."

He went into the other room and she sagged back against the kitchen counter. Though she'd known better, part of her had hoped he wouldn't be quite so agreeable. It would have made her feel better if he'd been a little more reluctant to break things off between them.

But that merely showed her instincts were right. The two of them couldn't make it work, so they might as well part on good terms and avoid the fights and broken hearts.

Except she was pretty sure her heart was already at least cracked.

11

"SO HOW was the trip out?"

In all the excitement of finally reaching San Diego, finding Susan's apartment and reconnecting with her old friend, Marlee had managed to avoid this question until the day after their arrival, when she and Susan were alone. Now the two of them were seated on the floor in Susan's living room, making rice bags to hand out to the wedding guests. It was the kind of busywork that invited sharing confidences.

Not that Susan's question wasn't perfectly innocent. She might have been merely making conversation. But Marlee knew Susan well enough to know that her friend was about to launch into full interrogation mode. Something about the look of avid interest in Susan's eyes, or the way she seemed on the verge of laughing, made Marlee wary. "Oh, it was fine. Long."

"But not exactly boring, huh?" Susan nudged Marlee in the ribs, then reached past her for another square of tulle.

"I didn't think people threw rice at weddings anymore," Marlee said, hoping to change the subject. She wasn't ready to talk about Craig yet. She was too confused about her feelings for him and what, if anything, she should—or could—do about them.

"You know me—I'm just an old-fashioned girl."

Marlee couldn't hold back a snort of laughter as she stared at her friend, who had bright red hair, four piercings in each ear, a tattoo on her ankle and had been the first in their circle of friends to try bungee-jumping. Some old-fashioned girl!

Susan started laughing, too. "Okay, so maybe it's just that rice is cheap and the church said they didn't care one way or another." She tied a thin green ribbon around the bundle of tulle-wrapped rice and reached for another square of fabric. "But don't change the subject. What's going on with you and Craig? I read on your blog that you had a fight. What was that about?"

"Oh, nothing important." She waved the question away.

"So did you kiss and make up?"

Marlee concentrated on tying the ribbon into a perfect little bow. "Sort of. We agreed to be friends."

"Just friends?"

She looked up at Susan. "Yes, just friends. Weren't you the one who said a romantic relationship between us would never work?"

"Of course it wouldn't. You are way too different." Susan dumped a scoop of rice into the middle of a round of netting. "Though he is kind of cute, isn't he?"

Yeah, like the Pacific kind of has a few waves. "He's fine." As in mighty fine, awesome fine, very fine indeed. The memory of exactly how fine made her squirm in her seat.

"He must have been pretty good to earn the title 'Magic' Chef."

"I, um, don't really want to talk about Craig right now."

"Why not?" Susan touched her arm. "It sounded

like the two of you were getting along so well. What happened?"

"Not any one thing, really. It's just..." She shrugged.

"Just what?" Susan pushed aside the pile of tulle and scooted closer to Marlee. "I'm not being nosy—I really care. And maybe talking it out will help you."

Marlee nodded. It would feel good to talk to someone. And maybe Susan could help her make sense of her tangled-up feelings. "Everything was fine as long as we were only having fun, you know?"

"You mean as long as you were just sleeping together with no plans to get serious?"

"Well, yeah. I mean, you know how when people go on vacation they do crazy stunts they'd never do at home, like get their hair braided or wear a thong bikini? Having a fling with Craig was my crazy stunt." She shrugged. "That makes me sound pretty shallow, I guess, but that's about the size of it."

"Hey, men have done it for centuries. Why shouldn't women have fun, too?"

"I guess you're right." Marlee picked up a strip of ribbon and wound it in and out of her fingers. "Anyway, the fact that we were so different didn't really matter when things weren't serious between us."

Susan's eyebrows rose. "But then things got serious?"

She felt all fluttery inside and took a deep breath, trying to quiet the sensation. "I thought I was really handling things well, not letting myself think any further than that night or maybe the next day, but then I realized that I was starting to think of the two of us as a couple next week and next month, even next year."

"Pretty normal, if you ask me."

"Yes, but I'd promised myself I wasn't going to let that happen with him. I mean, we *are* so different."

She looked down and discovered she'd tied the ribbon in a knot.

Susan nodded. "Of course, they do say opposites attract."

She tossed the knotted ribbon aside. "But Craig and I aren't opposite in a good way. We're bad for each other."

"Marlee Renee Jones! Shame on you. How could you possibly be bad for anyone?"

Susan's belief in her was touching. She actually had to swallow a knot of tears before she could speak. "That's sweet of you to say, but we could have died out there in the desert—all because I thought it would be fun to take off on some wild-goose chase, looking for a museum. And then I was too stubborn to stop and ask for directions."

"Even if you'd stopped, no one was home, so what was the point?"

"The point is, I realized Craig was right when he said I was irresponsible and immature. I need to make some changes in my life, do some growing up, before I can think about marrying anybody."

"*Marrying?* Who said anything about marrying?"

Marlee covered her mouth with her hand. She hadn't meant for that to slip out. She hadn't even dared *think* the *M*-word before now.

Susan leaned toward her, staring into her eyes. "You really fell in love with him, didn't you?"

Marlee nodded, afraid if she dared to open her mouth again she'd burst out sobbing.

Susan patted her shoulder. "I'm sure it's not as bad as you think. Craig didn't act like he blamed you at all for what happened. You couldn't have predicted that belt would break, after all."

"He was only being nice. The point is, while we

were walking back toward that house, risking sunstroke, I thought a lot about my life. I realized going with the flow all the time like I do is a sign of laziness. I've let life happen to me instead of making decisions for myself."

Susan frowned. "But you've been happy, haven't you? I mean, things seem to have worked out well for you."

"I've had some fun, sure. And mostly, I've been happy. But maybe I could be happier." Marlee sat up straighter, finally finding words for all the ideas she'd mulled over during the last couple of days. "My job, for instance. I've got the talent to plan bigger campaigns, to work with more important clients. But no one's ever given me the chance."

"They do take advantage of you. I've always thought that."

"But I've never asked for more responsibility, have I? And I've never stood up to my boss and told him not to dump all the crummy jobs on me." She sat up straighter. "The first thing I'm going to do when I get back to D.C. is have a talk with him. I'm going to ask for more challenging work, and a raise."

"There you go. That doesn't sound like an irresponsible, immature person to me."

Her shoulders sagged again. "That doesn't mean Craig and I could have any kind of future together. After all, he's still a by-the-book, very focused, serious kind of man."

"You mean he's anal and uptight. Didn't I warn you?"

She frowned. "Well, yeah. Though he did loosen up a little along the way. I mean, he went with me to the Wizard of Oz Museum, and he would have gone to the Desert Museum, if we had ever found it."

"Then doesn't that prove he's willing to bend a little for you?"

"Maybe… But I'm afraid he was only being so agreeable because we'd slept together and you know how guys are when there's sex involved."

Susan nodded. "Yeah. I see what you mean. But that usually wears off and their brains eventually move north again."

"And that's usually a good thing, but I'm afraid with Craig it would mean that we'd annoy each other that much more. I'm always going to be more relaxed and open to things than he is and he's always going to be Mr. Uptight."

"And you're just trying to avoid getting hurt any worse." Susan nodded. "I guess I should admire you for being smart enough to get out of a bad situation."

"Right." If only she could convince herself that staying away from Craig *was* smart.

"Maybe I can help you cheer up. At the rehearsal tonight I'll introduce you to Marcus."

Marcus? Oh yeah, the fix-up. "I don't know if that's such a good idea…." She wasn't ready to jump right into dating someone else. In fact, she didn't think she'd feel like dating again for a long time.

"Aww, c'mon. At least get to know him a little before you reject him outright. He's a great guy. He's a musician. He plays in an alt-rock band that has gigs in clubs all over San Diego."

"That's interesting." Any other time, the idea of dating a musician—someone creative, not part of the mainstream, corporate world—would have appealed to her. But a certain handsome chef had her thinking differently about everything these days.

"He's got a great sense of humor, and he's really cute—a great guy."

"If he's so perfect, why don't you go out with him?"

Susan laughed. "He's not as perfect as Bryan, of course. And he's not really my type. But I thought for you…"

"But he lives here, and I live in D.C."

"Long-distance relationships are very romantic. They keep things fresh." She added a completed rice bag to the growing pile in front of her. "Besides, he has family in Alexandria, so he's out there several times a year. And if you two get together, it will give you another reason to come out and see me more often."

"I have to get my license back first."

"Well, there is that. And we'd have to make sure you didn't get lost driving out here. But maybe he'll agree to come see you most of the time. And if you really hit it off and decide to get engaged, he can move to the east coast. Or better yet, you can move out here."

"Susan! I haven't even met the man yet and you're planning the wedding."

Susan's smile was a tad smug. "Just thinking positive. Something you always advocate, don't you?"

"Yeah." Except Marlee wasn't feeling very positive at the moment.

"I thought you said you were going to start being smarter," Susan reminded her. "I think it would be smart to meet someone new right away, and get Craig off your mind."

"Maybe so." Maybe a new man would help her get Craig off her mind. But she didn't think anyone could help her get him out of her heart.

"YOU'VE BEEN pretty quiet since you got here," Bryan said to Craig as the bartender set two beers in front of them. "Catch me up with what's been going on with you."

"I've been keeping busy." Craig looked around the dark paneled interior of the sports bar. The two friends were ostensibly here to plan Bryan's bachelor party, but how much planning did a night of drinking and carousing take? He figured it was really just an excuse to get away from the frenzy surrounding the approaching wedding for a while.

"Are you still thinking about opening your own restaurant?" Bryan helped himself to a handful of pretzels.

"Yeah." Craig took a long sip of beer. "I've about decided to quit worrying about it and go for it."

"Whoa! That's wild talk coming from you." Bryan laughed. "But if anybody can make a go of it, you can. I still dream about some of the dishes you cooked for me last time I was in D.C. If you've got the money to make a start, why not do it?"

He looked into his glass. "My dad thinks I'm crazy, that I should stay where I'm at and enjoy the security."

"Your old man checks the weather forecast before he gets dressed every morning—and he lives in New Mexico. It's not like a sudden monsoon or blizzard is going to ruin his golf plans."

He nodded. That was his dad, all right. And despite all the other ways they weren't alike, he'd apparently inherited his father's tendency toward caution. "I've got some money put aside, and I've looked into getting a line of credit from my bank."

"Don't forget Small Business Administration loans. My sister knows all about those. I can put you in touch with her."

"That's good. I already know the suppliers I'll need, and I've been working on a menu."

"And advertising. That's key to getting the word out about a new place."

"Yeah, uh, I'll need that, too." Was Marlee still interested in working with him on that? She'd been sort of…distant since they'd arrived in San Diego.

When she'd made that speech about not expecting them to see much of each other in the future, he'd thought she meant *after* the wedding. He'd told himself she was being sensible. They both had busy lives. But even then, he'd already decided he would look her up in a year or two, when he was ready for a serious relationship. It would be interesting to see if they connected in the same way after some time apart.

But then they'd arrived in San Diego and he'd been stunned at how much her sudden indifference wounded him. Maybe it was because he was still shaken up from their experience in the desert.

He took another long drink. When he'd looked back and seen her swaying by the side of the road, his heart had almost stopped. He'd cursed himself for marching her out in the heat that way. It would have made more sense to leave her with the car while he went for help himself.

Of course, knowing Marlee she wouldn't have stayed at the car. So, just as well she was with him. For a pretty together grown woman she brought out protective instincts he hadn't even known he had.

"Have you listened to a word I just said?"

Bryan's question snapped Craig out of his reverie. He pushed aside his empty beer mug and turned to his friend. "Sorry. I guess I have a lot on my mind."

"Relax." Bryan signaled the bartender and glanced at Craig. "You want another beer?"

"No, thanks."

Bryan ordered for himself, then turned back to Craig. "You always did worry too much," he said. "Launching a restaurant is a big step, but you'll do great. After all, you made better grades than I did in college, and you're the youngest head chef in the history of the Senate Dining Room. An overachiever like you can't miss."

He winced. Marlee had called him an overachiever, too, but she hadn't meant it as a compliment.

"So what's up with you and Marlee?" Bryan accepted a new mug of beer and took a sip.

"What makes you think something's up with me and Marlee?" Craig pretended interest in the appetizer menu posted behind the bar.

"Susan said she thought you two were an item. Something she read in that blog of Marlee's."

That blog. What would possess a woman to share her life with strangers that way? Then again, you had to admire a person who had nothing to hide. "I'm not sure what's happening with us," he said.

"Are you going to find out?"

"Maybe." He swiveled around and leaned back against the bar. "Maybe after the restaurant is up and running. That's going to take a lot of work. Since she's in advertising, I'm thinking I can ask her to help me with that and we'll see where it goes from there."

"Uh-huh. That's a nice safe plan."

"You don't think it's a good plan?"

Bryan raised both hands in a defensive gesture. "Hey, there's nothing wrong with it. It's exactly what I'd expect you to do. But from what Susan's told me about Marlee, she doesn't sound like a gal who would really appreciate the 'safe' approach."

"Oh, so you're about to get married and that makes you an expert."

"I'm just saying that Marlee seems like a real 'live

in the moment,' 'go for the gusto' woman. I'm not so sure that kind of chick will want to wait around for you to get your restaurant up and running smoothly before you decide whether or not you want to get serious with her. While you're working overtime and watching the bottom line she's liable to be out looking for somebody who wants to be with her now."

The thought tied his gut in knots. "It's not that I don't want to be with her, but now's not a good time for me to be getting seriously involved with anyone."

"So maybe Marlee isn't the gal for you. Or maybe in a few months or a year or so, when the restaurant's doing well, you can look her up and she'll be free and you two can pick things up where you left off."

That was a lot of maybes. He wished he'd taken Bryan up on that offer of another beer. Or maybe something stronger. He cleared his throat. "So you think if I'm interested in keeping things going with Marlee I should make my move now?"

Bryan shrugged. "It's up to you, dude. I guess it depends on how bad you want her."

How bad did he want her? He turned and signaled the bartender. Not that he was an expert on this kind of thing, but the feeling in his gut right now told him the answer to that question was…bad.

WHAT IS IT with these people who have all these definite plans for their future? I mean, talk to them and they've got the rest of their lives laid out as neatly as a menu. How do they know this stuff?

Obviously, I was in the ladies' room when they handed out that information. (Probably why I have no physical sense of direction, either.)

Or maybe they're all faking. I'm thinking that must be it. Because no way in the world do I know *what I'm supposed to do tomorrow much less for the rest of my life.*

This was never a really big problem before because I figured, hey, if you wake up each morning not expecting much, you could be in for a pleasant surprise. And I had a lot of fun.

But now that I've decided to be all responsible I figure that means making plans for my life and frankly, I don't have a clue. I can think of ten dozen things I'd like to do, but actually figuring out the steps to do them takes all the fun out of it, you know?

Of course, there's my job. I can start there. Time to start moving up the ladder and to tell you the truth, I can get with that program. I can see now that I was being lazy and letting my boss take advantage of me, but no more.

So, career taken care of. Check. Then there's the personal stuff, a much deeper swamp if you must know. And let's face it, my track record with the opposite sex is not exactly stellar. I've always complained about men who didn't want to make a commitment but I can see now that perhaps I came across as the type of woman who wasn't all that interested in permanence and long-term relationships myself. I didn't act very serious, so guys naturally thought I wasn't.

I'm going to try and do better in that area. But I tell you—this turning over a new leaf is really tough.

12

MARLEE WAS UNNERVED to find herself seated next to Craig at the wedding rehearsal dinner. She hadn't seen much of him since they'd arrived in San Diego, since he was staying with Bryan at his apartment and she was bunking with Susan. The strength of her response to him after two days' absence stunned her. Her heart pounded, she had trouble catching her breath and she felt lightheaded. She might have thought she was coming down with something if not for the fact that her hormones also got into the act, so that she was both turned on and annoyed. *Come on*, she thought. *This is not the time for this!*

Craig, of course, looked as calm and cool as ever. He smiled and held her chair for her. She mumbled her thanks and sat down, too wobbly legged to remain standing. "You look really nice," he said.

She smoothed the skirt of her red Chinese-silk mini dress. "Thanks. So do you." Dressed in a dark suit with a collarless white shirt he looked sexy as all getout. She fumbled with her silverware and reminded herself there was no sense getting all worked up about this man when nothing was going to come of it.

"I guess you've been busy helping Susan with all her last-minute preparations," Craig said as he unfolded his napkin into his lap.

"Yes, she's keeping me busy." She took a sip of

water. Did the restaurant people not realize how warm it was in here?

"I was thinking after this is over we might take a few days to drive up the coast. It should be beautiful this time of year."

"Uh-huh." She reached for a bread stick from the basket in front of her, then froze. *We?* What was he talking about? Hadn't they already decided there wasn't a *we?*

She cleared her throat. "Um, I've decided I'm going to go ahead and fly back home."

"Fly? But I thought you were afraid to fly."

"I am." She took a deep breath. "But it's time I got over that, don't you think? I mean, I'm a sensible, mature woman. I can do something thousands of other people do every day."

He didn't look particularly happy about this news. "I'd be happy to give you a ride back to D.C. I mean, there's no reason we can't still be friends."

"Of course we're still friends." Was there any greater fiction in romance? As if you could go from giving your heart and soul to someone to discussing the weather. And what happened when said former lover latched on to a new girl? A true "friend" would be enthralled by all the details of the new attachment, while Marlee had a feeling she'd be more inclined to want to rip the unfortunate female to shreds. "But I know you originally intended to use your time driving to work on all your plans for the restaurant. Now you can do that."

"Yeah. I guess I did."

What did it say about her as a person that she felt almost *happy* that he looked so disappointed? Maybe he did feel something for her....

And maybe tomorrow she'd win the lottery.

"Marlee!" Susan swooped down between them, a

wild look in her eyes. "What are you doing sitting here? You're supposed to be at the other end of the table, next to *Marcus*."

She looked down the table at a slight man with a goatee and glasses seated next to a woman who was old enough to be his grandmother. In fact, Marlee thought it might *be* Susan's grandmother. Marcus smiled and nodded at her. She looked back at Susan. "My place card was here."

Susan frowned. "How did that happen? I put your place card down there."

Craig coughed. Both women stared at him. "Something…went down the wrong way," he rasped, grabbing for his water glass.

Susan turned to Marlee again. "You can move, can't you?"

"But I've already started eating." Besides, she didn't want to move. She liked being near Craig, even if nothing would come of it.

"But I wanted you to meet Marcus."

"I'll meet him after dinner. I promise."

Still frowning, Susan looked from Marcus to Marlee and back again. "I suppose that's all we can do. All right."

She left them and Marlee tried to concentrate on her plate, aware of Craig watching her. "What was that all about?" he asked.

"Susan wants to fix me up with one of the groomsmen." She glanced toward Marcus, who was still watching her, a goofy smile on his face. Did Susan really think she'd like someone who smiled like that?

"Why would she want to do that?"

She shrugged. "Susan has this idea that she's a matchmaker. But her matches never work. That doesn't stop her from trying, though."

"And she thought this Marcus guy would be right for you?"

Marlee stirred a fork through her peas. "Yeah, well he's a musician and I guess she thought that would appeal to me."

"Does it appeal to you?"

"No. Yes. I don't know." The only man who appealed to her right now was sitting beside her. Impossible.

"He looks goofy to me."

She smiled at his choice of words. "Maybe he is. But then, I'm goofy myself sometimes."

"No, you're playful and endearing. There's a difference."

She looked at him in wonder. "Do you really think that?"

He cleared his throat and focused his attention on his plate. "I think I'm a pretty good judge of people."

And did he think "playful and endearing" were positive qualities in a woman? Qualities in someone he'd like to know better in the future?

She sat up straighter and forced her mind away from such fantasies. They'd already settled this. She and Craig were headed in different directions. A romance between the two of them would be a disaster.

Somehow she got through the rest of the meal, though she barely touched the food. When it was over and time to move on to the wedding rehearsal itself, Craig again held her chair for her. She was about to move past him when he touched her arm and leaned toward her. "Just so you know," he said softly, his breath stirring her hair in a way that made her heart race. "I switched the place cards."

"ALL RIGHT, everyone, let's run through the recessional again."

Craig stifled a groan. He was all for planning, but everyone had been to weddings before—why did they need to rehearse things over and over? Not to mention every time he took Marlee's arm to escort her down the aisle he got a feeling in his chest as though he'd swallowed a balloon.

He was pretty sure she felt it, too, since she refused to look at him. He glanced down at the top of her head, where her scalp showed white through the part of her dark hair, and fought the urge to kiss her there. This awkwardness between them was miserable, but he didn't know what to do about it.

He missed talking to her. Missed her smiling at him. Missed holding her. How was it in one week she'd gotten under his skin like this?

They stopped at the back of the chapel and turned to watch Susan and Bryan make their way down the aisle. He leaned over and whispered to Marlee. "Seems funny that we'd spend this much time rehearsing the wedding, and no one spends any time at all rehearsing being married."

She glanced at him. "Some couples live together before they get married."

"Yeah, but I don't think it's the same. Do you? There's not that promise of ''til death do us part' hanging over you."

She frowned. "You make it sound like a jail sentence or something."

"I don't really mean it that way, but it's a big promise to make, don't you think? What if you make a wrong choice? People do."

"But what if you make the right one?"

There went his chest again. Filling up with—something. It scared him a little, this sensation of not being in control of his feelings. "I should have known you'd say that," he told her. "You're such an optimist."

"What's wrong with that?""

"Nothing." He shook his head. "In fact, sometimes I wish I had your outlook on life."

Her expression softened and she patted his arm. "You're worried about your restaurant, aren't you?"

He hadn't been thinking about the restaurant at all, but he nodded anyway.

"Have faith in yourself. I know you can do it."

Her faith in him touched him. He was about to tell her as much when Susan's mother summoned them to the front of the chapel again. "I want to go over everyone's entrances again," she said.

A chorus of groans greeted this news, but they obediently trudged to their places once more. Craig and Bryan led the way from the anteroom at the side of the chapel, the two other groomsmen following. They took their places to the right of the altar and turned to watch the bridesmaids stutter-step down the aisle.

"By the time this is over, I am definitely going to be ready for the bachelor party," Bryan leaned over and mumbled to Craig.

Craig nodded. He was in the mood for a little mental oblivion himself. Anything to shake the black mood that had followed him around ever since Marlee had announced she was flying back to D.C. Alone.

He watched Marlee walk toward him down the aisle, the emptiness inside him expanding with each step she moved closer. What was wrong with him? He usually had a better grip on himself.

The organist switched to the wedding march and Susan came toward them. Craig glanced at Bryan.

His buddy's face practically glowed with happiness, and his huge grin would have been goofy if it wasn't so heart-felt.

The preacher did a quick run-through of the vows. Craig watched Marlee. She was hanging on every word, all that stuff about for richer or poorer, for better or worse. It seemed a lot for two people to juggle. Not only did you have to deal with all the stuff that went into living with another person, you still had to take care of the rest of your life.

He was a man who preferred to tackle one set of problems at a time. He'd gotten his education and his training out of the way; now it was time to get his business established. Then he could think about a serious relationship and marriage. Once that was stable, it would be time for children.

It was a sensible and logical approach. Anything else felt too risky.

"What's wrong with you, man? Get moving." Bryan nudged him. "I want to get out of here before the bars close."

He looked up and discovered they were recessing again. Marlee had stopped two steps down the aisle, waiting for him. "I think we're supposed to go together," she reminded him.

He nodded and took her arm. "Right. I ought to be able to remember that." It was simple on the surface. Why did his feelings have to make it so hard?

IF IT WEREN'T the night before the wedding, Marlee would gladly strangle Susan. Immediately after the rehearsal, the bride-to-be had dashed off to the bar where all the bridesmaids had agreed to meet, leaving Marlee to catch a ride with Marcus, who just happened to appear conveniently at her side the moment she discovered the others had left without her.

"I told Susan I'd get you there safe and sound," he said, grinning at her. He had prominent front teeth that showed below his moustache, giving him the appearance of a skinny rodent. A hamster maybe, or a squirrel.

"Aren't you going to the bachelor party?" She craned her neck to look over his shoulder, hoping to catch sight of someone else she could ride with.

"I'll catch up with everyone later. I'd much rather talk to you."

So he talked. All the way to the bar he talked. About the songs he wrote, and the guitars he'd played and the famous people he'd met. "I ran into Joe Pesci in the men's room at this little place over on the east side of town. The man is so cool ice practically drips off him."

And you are so boring I'm having to pinch myself to stay awake. She smiled weakly and nodded. "Are we almost to the bar?" she asked.

His grin transformed into a buck-toothed leer. "Worried you're going to have to leave me already? You know we could always blow off the parties and go off on our own. Get to know each other a little better." *He actually wagged his eyebrows!*

"No!" She cleared her throat. "I mean, I'm the maid of honor. I couldn't let Susan down that way."

"Yeah, I guess you're right." He sagged against the seat, temporarily deflated. "Chicks tend to get upset about that kind of thing don't they?"

"Yes," she said frostily. "Chicks do."

When he pulled up to the club, she couldn't get the passenger door open fast enough. "Thanks. See you later," she called over her shoulder as she raced for the front door, half afraid he'd follow her and try to drag her back to the car.

She found Susan and the others at a long table at the back of the room. "There you are!" Susan called over the throbbing music and motioned to a chair she'd saved next to her. "How did it go with Marcus?" she asked as Marlee dropped into the chair.

"Don't you *ever* pull a stunt like that again," she said, stashing her purse underneath the chair.

Susan looked dismayed. "You two didn't hit it off?"

"No, we did not." She flagged down a passing waitress and ordered a gin and tonic.

"Why not? What's wrong with him? I thought you two would have so much in common."

"Susan!" She glared at her friend. "He's a self-centered, boring, full-of-himself *squirrel*."

Susan frowned. "Now, I think that's a little harsh."

She shook her head. "I don't like him. Give it up."

"I think the real problem is you're still hung up on Craig."

Marlee flinched. "Maybe."

Susan leaned closer, her tone confidential. "I noticed him watching you all through the rehearsal. Maybe the attraction goes both ways."

She tried to push back the elation that swelled in her at this suggestion. When the waitress set her drink in front of her, she grabbed it and took a big gulp. "We already agreed that it didn't make sense for us to keep seeing each other."

"So un-agree. Tell him you've changed your mind."

"It's not that easy. What if I'm reading him wrong? What if he thinks I'm this unstable woman who can't even make a decision and stick to it?"

"What if the sky falls tomorrow?" Susan nudged her. "Since when have you been afraid of laying it all on the line? How are you going to know what will happen unless you try?"

"Right." She took another sip of her drink. It was easy enough to talk about "laying it all on the line." Much harder to do when the "all" was your suddenly very-fragile-feeling heart.

CRAIG SAT at the bar, nursing an oversize drink, scarcely aware of the mostly naked woman gyrating on the stage a few inches away. While Bryan's other friends hollered and laughed and took turns slipping dollar bills into the dancer's G-string, he sank deeper into a black funk.

As he'd driven away from the church tonight, he'd seen Marlee getting into a car with one of the groomsmen, Marcus. The guy Susan had been trying to fix her up with. Apparently, she'd decided he wasn't so bad after all.

He'd noticed Marcus wasn't with them at the bar. Were he and Marlee somewhere together?

He groaned and slugged back the rest of his drink. Someone clapped him on the back and he looked up into Bryan's flushed face. "What's wrong with you?" Bryan asked.

"Nothing's wrong with me."

"Then how come you aren't joining in the fun?" He fanned a fistful of dollar bills in front of his face. "These ladies are working for tips you know. It wouldn't be right not to reward them for all their hard work."

He glanced at the woman on the stage. She was gyrating around a pole, a vacant, bored look on her face. "She doesn't look too thrilled to be here to me," he said.

"More thrilled than you are, that's for sure." Bryan

slid into an empty chair next to him. "So what is it? Are you nervous about tomorrow?"

"Nervous? Why should I be nervous?"

"I know you're not much for speaking in public."

"Speaking in p—? Oh, the toast." He nodded. He'd forgotten it was traditional for the best man to toast the couple. "Don't worry, I can handle it." If push came to shove, he could always stand up and wish Bryan and Susan a happy future together. Short and sweet. Nobody wanted to listen to the best man at these things anyway. It was one of those formalities of etiquette the mother of the bride was so set on. "Don't worry, I won't let you down," he said.

Bryan clapped him on the back again. "That's my man. Now come on, have some fun."

"Bryan, over here. You gotta see this!"

The groom drifted away to join the rest of the party. Craig looked at his empty drink glass and thought about ordering another, then decided against it. He stood and headed toward Bryan and the others, but stopped before he reached them. This was ridiculous. He wasn't in a party mood, and all he was doing was spoiling everyone else's fun.

He worked his way over to Bryan and leaned close to talk to him. "Listen, Bry, I'm going to cut out early."

"You are?" Bryan looked around the attractive waitress who had arrived with another tray full of drinks. "Why?"

"I think I'd better go work on my toast for tomorrow."

"Oh. Okay. If you really think you have to."

"I do." Craig manufactured a smile for his friend. "Have a great time. I'll see you tomorrow."

"Okay." He'd already turned back to the waitress and the others.

He walked out into the parking lot, and found his car. As he slid into the front seat, the shiny figure hanging from the rearview mirror caught his eye. The Tin Man. The one who'd been searching for a heart on the journey to Oz.

Why a heart? He wracked his brain, trying to remember the details of the story. Something about believing love was the most important thing a person could have.

He caught his breath, and fumbled to insert the key in the ignition. It slipped from his hand and he bent down, groping on the floor for it. His hand encountered something soft and round. He straightened and came up with the set of juggling balls, still in their net bag.

He stared at the brightly colored balls, remembering the look on Marlee's face when she'd bought them for him. She'd had such faith in him—faith that he could do anything. Did she still think that? Or was that part of the fantasy, too—part of their "fling" as she insisted on calling it, something that couldn't carry over into their everyday lives?

SUSAN and Bryan's wedding day dawned clear and warm. As Marlee helped Susan dress for the ceremony, she told herself she wasn't going to cry. It was such a cliché, sobbing during the wedding. Not to mention tears would make her mascara run and she'd have raccoon eyes.

But how could she not cry with happiness for her friend? Susan looked so gorgeous in her wedding dress and veil, and Bryan looked so overjoyed when she started down the aisle. What she wouldn't give to have a man look at her that way!

So Marlee sniffed and dabbed her way through

the vows, telling herself it was just as well she'd shed a few tears because now everyone would think her eyes were red from the crying and not because she'd hardly slept the night before. Only the judicious use of heavy-duty concealer kept her from looking like a hag.

Of course, she could use the excuse that she'd partied until the wee hours with the rest of the bridesmaids and Susan, but they'd actually packed it in early. She'd ended up tossing and turning all night, trying to convince herself she'd done the right thing by turning down Craig's offer to give her a ride back to D.C. Not only did the thought of getting on a plane and flying across country send cold chills down her spine, she'd had to admit that no matter how many times her brain told her Craig was not the man for her, her heart and hormones begged to differ.

As for Craig, one of the ushers had reported that he'd spent most of the bachelor party stressing over the toast he had to make at the wedding dinner. Halfway through the night, he'd apparently taken off, saying he had a lot of practicing to do.

Typical Craig, worrying about being perfect.

If only he knew how perfect she already thought he was.

By the time she took her place at the front of the wedding chapel alongside the other bridesmaids, she had almost persuaded herself to tell him she'd changed her mind and wanted to make the trip back to D.C. with him. If one week in close quarters had created these kind of feelings in her, who knew what another week would do?

But she'd pushed the thought away. The week they'd spent together had been a fun fantasy, but it was time to get back to real life. A real life where she definitely needed to make some changes. She'd start by getting on that plane tomorrow.

Once the ceremony was over, she and Susan hugged, and she kissed Bryan on the cheek, which seemed to please him. Then the photographer rounded them all up for pictures. The entire wedding party. Only the women. Best man and maid of honor with the bride and groom. All the attendants. Marlee's face hurt from smiling so much.

"We need a shot of the maid of honor and the best man together," Susan said.

Marlee made a face at her friend. "I don't really think—"

"All right, you two, stand together there in front of the flowers." The photographer motioned them into place. "Now the best man put your arm around her shoulder. That's nice. Now smile...."

The bright flash left spots dancing in her vision and she swayed. Craig steadied her. "You okay?"

"Yeah, just tired of taking pictures." She raised one foot and then the other. "And my feet hurt."

"Take your shoes off."

The suggestion surprised her, coming from him. "In church?"

He smiled. "No one will care. And your dress is long, so who'll see?"

She slipped out of the high-heeled pumps. "Think they'll notice I'm suddenly three inches shorter?"

"I won't point it out if you won't."

They smiled at each other, and the familiar longing filled up her heart again. Too bad things hadn't worked out.... She'd have to ask Susan for a copy of the picture of them together, if only to remember what might have been.

The reception was a formal sit-down dinner at a

country club. Marlee sat across from Craig at the table for the wedding party. She tried not to look at him, but he was so handsome in his tux that her gaze kept drifting back to him. She went through the motions of eating and counted the minutes until she could safely make an exit. The food, some sort of chicken dish, looked beautiful, but she couldn't have told anyone if it was good or if it tasted like rubber.

"Is something wrong?" Craig leaned across the table and whispered to her.

"Wrong?" She blushed. "No. Nothing's wrong. Why would you think something's wrong?"

"The way you were staring at me, I thought maybe I had lettuce in my teeth or something."

"No, you look great."

Susan's mother stopped behind his chair and put her hand on his shoulder. "Craig, I believe now would be a good time for your toast," she said.

"Right." He laid aside his napkin and stood. Mrs. St. John tapped a spoon against her wineglass and the murmur of conversation stilled. Craig cleared his throat.

"Congratulations to Susan and Bryan. Watching them together, it's plain to see how much they love each other. It isn't easy to find that kind of love in today's world. There are a lot of things competing for a couple's time and energy."

He paused, and Marlee was shocked to realize he was overcome by emotion. Was it the idea of his best friend tying the knot that moved him so. Or was he, like Marlee, thinking of what might have been between them?

He cleared his throat and raised a glass of champagne. "Susan and Bryan have found the real thing— the kind of love that can stand up to the trials and tribulations of the real world. A love that will stand the test of time. Here's to you both, wishing you a lifetime of happiness together."

As clinking glasses rang like chimes throughout the dining room, Marlee pressed her napkin to her mouth and choked back a sob. While everyone's attention was focused on the happy couple, she fled to the ladies' room and locked herself in a stall, sobbing into a wad of toilet paper. Craig's words had been so beautiful. Why couldn't she have found a love like that with him, instead of a fragile fantasy that would never hold up against the pressures of everyday life?

13

SOMEHOW I survived the flight from San Diego to D.C. Six hours suspended in the air and I thought it would never end. I'm not ashamed to say that I made it only with the help of multiple bloody Marys and the relaxation CD dear Susan gave me before she left on her honeymoon.

Unfortunately, give me enough to drink and I turn maudlin. By the time we were over Kansas City I'd soaked through three cocktail napkins and the man seated next to me was seriously alarmed. He finally worked up the nerve to ask what was wrong.

I told him I was flying home from a funeral and he was kind enough to buy me another bloody Mary.

MARLEE certainly felt as if she were in mourning—not for a person, but for a relationship. Had she totally blown it by giving up so soon on being with Craig? Or had she done the mature thing breaking it off?

By the time the plane landed she'd halfway convinced herself that she'd been duped by the whole compressed nature of her relationship with Craig. That, and the fact that for five days they'd pretty much spent every second together and hadn't had much to do with anyone else. So of course her emotions and her thinking were all out of whack. All she needed was to get back to the real world and she'd be thinking clearly again in no time.

Unfortunately, her real world included the ever-growing pile of P.I.O. sheets in her office. Somehow, in her absence, the stack she'd relegated to the corner had doubled in size. On top was a faded orange pamphlet titled Maintaining a Safe Fallout Shelter. She glared at it for a while, but when that didn't make it go away, she went in search of Gretchen.

"Oh, hi, Marlee. Are you back already?" Gretchen looked up from the stapler she was refilling.

Not exactly an enthusiastic greeting. "I got back into town last night."

"Did you have a nice time?"

Nice was such a lame word, wasn't it? An afternoon with her parents might be nice. A good salad at lunch was nice. Her trip, on the other hand had been at times frustrating, thrilling, amazing, fantastic and heart-wrenching. Better ignore the question. It wasn't as if Gretchen was interested anyway. "What's up with all the P.I.O. sheets in my office?"

"Oh, Marty had a bunch in his office, too, so Gary told him to give them to you. I guess he thinks it's more efficient that way, having everything consolidated."

"But why does it have to be consolidated in *my* office?"

Gretchen's eyes widened in an attempt at an innocent look. "It has to be somewhere, doesn't it?"

Right. And she had to have some form of gainful employment. Her usual attitude had been to accept whatever work landed in her lap as her fate and go on, uncomplaining. Post-road-trip Marlee wasn't so complacent. "I really don't think my job is to rewrite P.I.O. sheets."

Gretchen shrugged. "You'll have to take that up with Gary."

"I will." Before she lost her nerve, she marched past Gretchen's desk and knocked on Gary's door.

"Come in."

Gary was hunched over his desk, frowning at a row of plastic drink glasses set out in front of him. "Which of these designs do you think would get the most attention at the summer barbecue for General Services employees?" he asked.

"Oh, uh, well, let's see." She came around his desk and studied the drink glasses, all of which bore variations of the firm's logo. "The pink one, I think. It's brightest."

He picked up the pink glass and considered it. "Yes, but how will the men feel about carrying around a pink glass? Does pink make us seem too feminine? And why do they call it a glass when it's really plastic?"

"I don't know, Gary. If you don't like pink, go with the orange."

"The orange, yes." He picked up the orange glass. "You don't think the logo is too small?"

"It's fine. Really. I need to talk to you for a minute."

He looked up at her and blinked. "Oh, hello, Marlee. I didn't realize you were back from your vacation."

Great how everyone had missed her so much.

"I wanted to talk to you about my job duties," she said.

"Job duties?" He frowned. "Are you referring to something in particular?"

Though he hadn't invited her, she sat in the chair across from his desk. "I've been here five years,

Gary. I think I've moved beyond rewriting P.I.O. sheets."

"But someone has to do them."

· "Why not give them to one of the interns? Or someone with less experience than me?"

"I didn't mean them as an insult." He opened a desk drawer and swept the glasses into it. "Everyone else is busy and you've always been so good about pitching in and doing whatever needs to be done."

Translation—I thought I could dump them on you and you wouldn't complain. "I want to do something more challenging."

"You do? I had no idea you were so ambitious."

Surprise, neither did I! She sat up a little straighter. Might as well go for broke. "And I want a raise."

Gary frowned. "As a non-profit, we really don't have the funds."

"You have money in the budget. I checked." She was stretching the truth a little here, but it was widely known that Gary prided himself on always operating under budget. He could afford to add a little to her paycheck without going into the red.

"I'll have to give this some consideration," he said. He picked up the phone. "If you'll excuse me, I have a call to make."

She stood. "You'll get back to me?"

"Of course, Marlee. In due time."

Going with the flow was definitely easier on the nerves than trying to steer her own course. As she headed back to her office, irritation at Gary's brush-off simmered. She collapsed into her desk chair and glared at the stack of P.I.O. sheets. She wondered if there was anything in there on career planning.

Or better yet, life planning.

ON WEDNESDAY, Marlee received a post card from Craig. On the front was a trio of saguaro cacti, each wearing an oversize sombrero. On the back he'd written:

Spent the night in a Comfort Lodge in Flagstaff. The Saguaro Sleep-Inn was across the street and I couldn't seem to resist checking it out for you. I give it a five on the kitsch-meter. Funny, I wouldn't have even noticed it before I met you. Makes me wonder what else I've been missing.

Craig

She clutched the postcard to her breast, stuck somewhere between laughing and crying. So Craig was still thinking about her.

As if he hadn't been crowding out most of her other thoughts since they'd climbed out of his car in San Diego. She told herself when work was going better she wouldn't think about him so much.

But work wasn't going all that well, either. Gary was obviously ignoring her, and she was so bored she'd resorted to making up ad campaigns for fictitious products:

Cramitall—the storage solution for everyone with too much stuff! Doubles your closet capacity. No need to part with out-of-style clothes or appliances you don't use. Cramitall, the perfect accessory for packrats everywhere!

The PMS Patch—The Premenstrual Measurement System lets friends, family and co-workers know where you are on the PMS scale. Soft pink—okay to approach. Deep purple—stay out of your way. And if the patch is black—watch out, you're armed and dangerous! When you can't deal with PMS, let others deal with you!

Makeup in Minutes—From those nights you stayed out too late, to those days when the zits are winning, simply slap on this pre-painted mask. Shapes to your face and shows the world a more glamorous you! More professional than a paper bag over your head. Extreme versions for disco night or Halloween!

Marlee sat down in front of the computer and tried to concentrate on actual work, such as a fund-raising flyer for a Kennedy Center concert to benefit the National Heart Association. But her thoughts kept drifting to saguaro cacti and a certain chef.

She clicked on her e-mail program.

From: Marlee@TWM.com
To: TopToque@govnet.net
Subject: happy trails to you
Hi Craig,
Thanks for the postcard. It has pride of place in my collection of kitsch, right next to my stuffed jackalope from the Dimitt general store.
 Hope your trip back home was uneventful.
Marlee

She hesitated over the sign off, her finger hovering over the *L* on her keyboard. At the last minute she decided she wasn't going to go there. No sense making things complicated.

She turned back to the phony copy file.

Heartbreak helper. One pill twice a day for six months and you'll feel better in no time. Severe cases may require longer treatment. Best taken in conjunction with our *Instant Amnesia Elixir.* Side effects may include sleeplessness and a fondness for sappy movies. This product is not guaranteed to be effective in severe cases.

CRAIG SKIMMED through the long list of unanswered e-mails on his laptop while he unpacked the ingredients for chicken corn chowder. After two weeks of road food he was craving a homemade meal. Not to mention that cooking was his outlet whenever he was stressed.

The trip back to D.C. had taken forever. He'd re-created his schedule as well as he could from memory, and had had no trouble sticking to it. The weather had been great and there'd been no delays due to traffic or road construction. Any other time, he would have thought the journey was perfect.

But that was before he'd met Marlee and discovered that detours and delays weren't always bad things, and that taking time to smell the roses—or a woman's floral perfume—definitely made life sweeter.

He spotted Marlee's e-mail address in his mailbox and thought at first his eyes were playing tricks on him. After all, she was pretty much all he'd thought about since leaving San Diego. Every night in another generic motel had been agonizingly long, his bed painfully empty without her beside him.

He clicked open the message and read it, smiling at her comment about his postcard. He'd thought she'd get a kick out of that. And he wanted her to know he was thinking of her.

That he missed her.

Dammit, that was the real problem. His life had been unfolding in perfect order before he met her, everything going according to plan. And then she'd stepped in like a bright-colored tornado and scattered his plans—and his peace of mind—to the four winds.

He read her message again, fighting down the hope spreading through his chest. Just because she'd written him didn't mean anything special. She'd made it clear he wasn't her type.

He punched the save button, then switched off the computer and focused on preparing the soup. As he diced onion and chopped chicken he made a mental list of everything he had to do: he needed to talk to the real estate agent about renting that space on Fifteenth Northwest he'd found, then make an appointment with the architect and the designer. He'd have to arrange inspections, hire staff, order supplies, design menus and plan advertisements.

The knife slipped, almost cutting his thumb. He cursed and stooped to gather up the pieces of onion that had scattered across the floor.

He'd counted on Marlee to do the advertising. He'd have to look for someone else now, but who else would get what he was trying to do here? Who else would have the kind of faith in him she'd have?

He scraped the onion into the trash and began chopping another. On the drive home, he'd decided to take Marlee's advice to heart—to go for his dream and take every chance he got. He'd vowed not to focus on what could go wrong, but to cherish everything that went right.

Going by that philosophy, how should he look at his failure with Marlee? As a lesson learned that he could take into his next relationship?

He shook his head and scraped the onions into a

pan of hot oil. He didn't want another relationship. He wanted Marlee.

He added garlic and green pepper to the pan and stirred it vigorously. *Think, Brinkman, what are you going to do?*

He watched the onion turn translucent and added two cups of chicken broth. As the concoction simmered and fragrant steam surrounded him, he went to the refrigerator for a pint of heavy cream.

Unfortunately, all he found was a quart of milk and some sour cream. He looked at the two containers, shrugged, and carried them to the stove. One rule of cooking was that when an ingredient wasn't available, you improvised.

As he stirred sour cream into the pan and added milk, he smiled. That was the answer to this whole Marlee dilemma. When one approach didn't work, you had to improvise.

Marlee thought they weren't compatible in their everyday lives. Here was his chance to prove her wrong—and realize his dream in the process.

HER SECOND Monday after returning from San Diego, Marlee was in her office trying to brainstorm something brilliant for a Stop Smoking campaign when Craig stuck his head around her door. "Is this the office of Marlee Jones, the talented marketing maven?" he asked.

She laughed, her heart jitterbugging in her chest at the sight of him. "More like Marlee Jones, marketing drudge."

He came in and sat down. "I brought you these." He handed her a white cardboard bakery box.

"What is it?" she asked as she lifted the lid.

"Madeleines. I made them myself."

"Oh, wow." They smelled divine—almost as wonderful as he looked. "That was sweet of you."

"Consider it a bribe. I need your help."

"You do?"

"I've decided to go ahead with my restaurant."

"Craig, that's wonderful! Congratulations."

He grinned. "Thanks. I'm pretty psyched. And nervous."

She set aside the cookies. "You'll do great. I know you will."

"I have a good location and suppliers lined up and I've planned a menu. But I need a good advertising campaign to make it happen. That's where you come in."

"It is?"

"You offered to help me, remember?"

"Of course I do. And I meant it. But are you sure you wouldn't rather have someone with more experience?"

He looked around her tiny office until his gaze came to rest on a poster showing a cascade of theatrical masks falling toward a trash can. Depression hides the real you read the caption, a campaign she'd designed for Mental Health Month a couple of years ago. "Is that your work?" he asked.

"Yes. One of my favorites."

"It looks good." His eyes met hers. "If you do as well for me, I'll be happy."

"I'd be thrilled to help you," she said. But she'd take it slow, and avoid getting her hopes up. After all, this was the real world now. Anything could happen.

GOOD NEWS, *everyone! The Magic Chef and I are making a go of it again and everything is full speed ahead for his restaurant. No name yet, so keep those ideas coming in. I'm in charge of advertising for the project, so I'll be busy putting everything together on that end.*

In fact, I'll be so busy I've decided to quit my job! You heard it here first. I'm thinking this restaurant gig could be the start of big things for me. I'm going to start my own company.

I plan to specialize in small businesses and new start-ups, so if you know anyone looking for terrific, creative marketing at reasonable prices, send them here!

MARLEE POSTED her latest blog entry, then sat back and watched her phone. Any minute now...

Brrrrring!

"Hello, Susan."

"What's all this about you and Craig? I thought that was over."

"He asked me to help him with the advertising for his restaurant."

"So this is strictly business?"

"Well...not exactly. We've sort of picked up where we left off after our road trip." There had been a few kisses, a few dinners and one memorable night together. "We're taking things slow."

"What does that mean?" Susan's voice rose. Marlee imagined her gripping the phone in white-knuckled frustration. "Is it serious?"

She shifted in her chair. "I think it could be. I mean, he made a point of looking me up and asking me to help him. That has to mean something, don't you think?" Craig wasn't the most demonstrative man she'd ever met, so she had to read between the lines, but she felt as if they were getting closer...to something. Something permanent, or at least long-term. But this was new territory for her, too, so she couldn't be sure. "We're seeing a lot of each other," she said. "And we're getting along great. Of course, he's really focused on the restaurant right now, but I have a really good feeling about things."

"I think you need to tell him that."

Marlee's stomach fluttered. "Tell him what?"

"Tell him that you want to be more than friends, or co-workers, or whatever you are. Tell him you love him, if that's what you're feeling."

The fluttering moved up her chest. She leaned forward, elbows on her desk. "Oh, I think it's too soon for that. Besides, I'm waiting for him to say something first."

"Then you could be waiting a long time." Susan's voice softened. "I know you're one for letting things happen in their own time, but sometimes you have to be more pro-active and make them happen. Maybe Craig needs a little push."

"I'm not really the pushy type." Marlee took a deep breath, determined to remain positive. "Everything will work out. You'll see." She had a good feeling about Craig. About the two of them as a couple. They both just needed a little more time.

MARLEE'S RESIGNATION did not result in wailing and gnashing of teeth. Not that she expected anyone to make a huge fuss, but it would have been nice if Gary had at least asked her to reconsider.

"What's this?" he asked, looking up from a row of golf balls lined up on the desk in front of him.

"It's my resignation," she said. "I quit."

"Don't be ridiculous." He turned his attention back to the golf balls. "Which of these do you think is best for the charity golf tournament next month?"

"I don't care, Gary. I quit."

He tore his attention from the golf balls once more. "Why?"

"I'm tired of this place and my dead-end job. I'm talented, you know." She held her head up. "I want the opportunity to challenge myself. To grow and learn and be better."

"You've never expressed anything like this before."

"What do you think I've been trying to do these past few weeks?"

"I thought it was a phase. A restlessness. After all, you just got back from a vacation, attending a friend's wedding. I was sure you'd have settled down by now."

"That's the problem. I'm too settled here. I'm giving my notice. I'll stay for two weeks to help train my replacement."

"Oh, I think a week will be enough." He began gathering golf balls and dropping them into his drawer. "What will you do?"

"I don't know." That was the scary part. The leap of faith part. But she'd come to believe if she didn't get out of this place she'd never be motivated to find someplace better. "I'm thinking of launching my own company."

"You're taking a big risk," Gary said. "Some might say you're being foolhardy."

"Maybe so, but it's something I have to do."

"All right. And good luck." He glanced up as she turned to leave. "About those P.I.O. sheets?"

"They're all yours, Gary."

"What are we going to do with those things?"

"Maybe you should take up origami."

There was an idea. She wondered what Craig would think of an origami theme for his restaurant. Paper cranes and frogs... That could work. Or maybe he'd prefer a folksier look, like all those diners they'd visited on their trip. There were so many possibilities. That's what made life—and love—so exciting.

AFTER her meeting with Gary, Marlee dashed into the former Vietnamese café that was being remodeled into Craig's new restaurant. He'd thrown himself into making his dream a reality and as a result they'd been limited to brief phone calls several times a day and a couple of hurried dinners on weekends. She still hadn't seen his apartment, though he'd spent one night at her place. It wasn't the ideal way to build a relationship, but when was real life ever ideal? They were working with what they had and so far, so good.

She hurried into the bar, where she found him frowning over a stack of ceramic tiles in different colors. The frown didn't leave his face when he saw her. "You're late," he said.

He was in his "intense" mode—the one in which he operated most of the time lately. It was also her least favorite of his moods, but one she was learning to handle. "Sorry. I had a meeting at work." Later, when he was in a better mood, she'd tell him her good news—that she was leaving her dead-end job and striking out on her own. She settled onto a bar stool and looked at the tiles. "Are these for the foyer?"

He nodded. "What color do you think? I like the black, because it says 'sophisticated,' but is it too dark?"

"That depends on your theme."

"My theme?" The worry lines on his forehead came together in a deep V.

"Sure. You need some kind of theme to serve as a starting point. Everything else grows from that—the decor, the menu, and of course, the advertising. So

the first thing we need to do is to decide on a theme."
She took a spiral notebook from her purse and readied herself to take notes.

He shook his head. "I don't think we need a theme. It's too gimmicky."

Of course he would say this. She managed not to sigh dramatically. "There's a difference between a theme and a gimmick, though sometimes they can be related."

"I want this to be a dignified, classy place."

"Then 'classy' can be your theme. But to a lot of people that says 'expensive.' You could be limiting your clientele."

"I don't want any limits. I want to serve good food in a nice atmosphere."

She shook her head. "*Nice* doesn't tell me anything. You need to be more specific. What do you want people to feel when they come here?"

"Hungry?" He shoved aside the tiles. "Look, I don't have time for this now. I have to get to the seafood market before they close."

"And I came all the way across town to meet with you so we could decide on the advertising campaign." In addition to being stubborn and controlling, was he going to be inconsiderate, too?

"You were late."

"I told you I couldn't help it." God, the man was so mule-headed! She wanted to shake him. "You should send someone else."

"As chef it's my responsibility to choose the fish myself."

"Haven't you heard of delegating?"

"It's my responsibility," he repeated stubbornly.

She set aside her notebook. "The thing is, you have no concept of balance."

"You're telling me you don't put your whole self into your work?"

"Not to the point where I don't have fun."

"Why does everything have to be fun?"

"Everything doesn't have to be, but eating out should be." And relationships should be. The Craig she'd traveled with had known how to relax and laugh at himself. The restaurant entrepreneur seemed to have forgotten that.

"I want people to come for the food."

Hadn't they covered this already? "The food will keep them coming, but a theme will get them here in the first place and help you stand out from the crowd."

"I don't know. I don't think like that. I'm too logical."

"And I'm illogical?" She was. She admitted it and was even proud of it, but that didn't mean he could use it against her. If they were going to argue, he had to fight fair.

"Not that. Just not…serious."

"Is that what you want—someone serious? Because I was under the impression that you wanted *me*."

"I do want you. But I need you to focus and get serious about helping me."

"No, you want someone to do what you want."

He folded his arms across his chest. "My reputation is the one on the line here."

"But you asked for my opinion and now you won't even listen to what I have to say."

"I *am* listening."

"No, you're not. You're arguing."

He unfolded his arms, fists clenched at his sides. "You're the one who's arguing. I happen to be right."

"You are not always right." She stood and stuffed the notebook back into her purse. "I thought you'd changed, that you'd learned how to relax and have fun. To be open to new ideas and new possibilities. But as soon as you crossed the D.C. line you turned back into the old, uptight Craig."

"I have changed. But obviously not as much as you'd like."

She slung her purse across her shoulder and faced him. "No, you haven't changed," she said. "You still put your own ideas and…and your precious *dignity* ahead of everything else!" She whirled and stalked out, waiting for him to follow, listening for him to call out to her, to apologize.

But she didn't hear anything. When she looked over her shoulder no one was following her. Then again, running after a woman on a downtown street wouldn't be *dignified* would it? It wouldn't be the *image* he wanted. People might think he'd *failed* at the relationship game.

She gritted her teeth, choking back a sob. The man was impossible. Hidebound, stick-in-the-mud, controlling, confounding and thoroughly irritating.

And in spite of all that, she loved him with all her heart. And she was dying inside, knowing he hadn't cared enough to come after her.

If only he'd bend even a little. If only he'd admit that he wasn't *always* right. She wasn't asking for a lot, just some proof that he cared more about her than his precious image or his precisely laid plans. She wanted some small acknowledgment that he was willing for them to work *together* on their relationship, instead of always being at odds and having to battle their way to a middle ground.

She wanted the old Craig back—the one she'd discovered on the way to San Diego—the guy who took her to the Wizard of Oz museum and sang along with the Rolling Stones on the car radio. That Craig had been fun and kind and…and *real*. More real than the control-Nazi who was stressing over this restaurant project, hung up on the idea that everything, including himself, had to be perfect.

If only she could find that other version of Craig again, the one she'd fallen in love with.

14

IF THIS were paper, dear friends, you'd see tear stains on these pages. Yes, my life has taken a sad detour of late, which I don't intend to go into here. (I love you all, but this is a public forum and certain people might read this and get the wrong impression. They might think I'm crying over them when I'm really crying over my own short-sightedness in thinking that certain people could ever really change.)

After all, changing one's mind, or one's life, is so undignified. *You might end up looking like a fool, instead of actually being one.*

And Susan, if you're reading this (and I know you are) don't call me. I don't want to talk about it.

MARLEE WAS CLEANING out her desk when Gretchen paged her. "Marlee, there's someone here to see you."

A friend would have walked on into her office, so it must be a client. Too bad. She leaned across a stack of files and punched the intercom button. "I don't work here anymore, Gretchen," she said. "Send them to someone else."

She was in no mood to be nice to a client today. In addition to having to clean out her office and worry about where her next paycheck was coming from, she hadn't heard one word from Craig since their fight at his restaurant last week.

At first, she hadn't thought the argument was that big a deal. She was sure he'd come around to her way of thinking. He'd call and apologize. They'd have a good talk and maybe even great make-up sex. That was the way things were with them—lots of fireworks, both good and bad. It wasn't like any other relationship she'd ever had, but she had been getting used to it.

But then he hadn't called or e-mailed or stopped by or…or anything. The knowledge was a cold hollow place in her heart. She grabbed her stuffed Smokey the Bear from the credenza and shoved it into a box, followed by a color wheel and a stack of plastic templates. Maybe she'd misjudged him. Maybe he was too stubborn to meet her in the middle. Maybe he'd decided she wasn't worth the effort.

She bit her lip and told herself she absolutely wasn't going to cry. Not here at the office. Later, at home, she might give in to a sob fest, but not here. Not where people might see her and think she was crying over this lousy job.

"You'd better come out here, Marlee." Gretchen's voice blared on the intercom again. "Now."

Sighing, she shoved aside the half-filled box and frowned toward the doorway. What was Gretchen up to? She hoped to God it wasn't some cheesy farewell party or something like that. She really wanted to leave quietly, without a fuss.

She looked around the room, but she hadn't uncovered any windows or other escape routes while she was packing, so she guessed she'd have to gut it up and go out there. She smoothed her hair, straightened her shoulders and prepared to fake a smile for whomever—or whatever—waited for her.

But all her bravado deserted her when she saw Craig standing by the reception desk. Gretchen, Gary and most of her co-workers were there, too. Had he summoned them as witnesses so she wouldn't be tempted to cut loose and let him have it when he officially dumped her? Wasn't that the strategy men used when they took their dates to an expensive restaurant before they called it quits?

She stopped a few feet away from him. "Craig. What are you doing here?"

"We didn't finish our conversation the other day," he said.

"I said all I have to say." She took a step back, weighing the merits of running back into her office and shutting the door. He'd have to leave eventually, wouldn't he? But then he'd think she was a coward. She was a lot of things, but yellow wasn't one of them.

"I've had some time to think and there are still a few things I want to get across." He set a small shopping bag on the reception desk—the kind of thing people used for takeout food.

"Did you bring lunch?" she asked, trying for a joke.

"No. Just a few...I guess you'd call them visual aids."

"Visual aids?" She sank onto the arm of the reception room sofa. What did he need visual aids for?

"I've been thinking a lot about us. About how much goes into a successful relationship. It's a real balancing act."

He paused and began taking things out of the bag. Marlee watched, fascinated, as he held up a small stuffed heart made of red satin. "First, you have your love for one another." He began tossing the heart in the air and catching it with one hand. "You have to balance that with your hopes and dreams for your lives together."

He held up a small figure. She gasped as she recognized the Tin Man air freshener. Craig began tossing this up and catching it with his other hand. "You have to balance all that with your career." He added a wooden spoon to the mix. The three objects arced through the air, deftly passed from hand to hand. Craig was juggling!

She grinned and began to clap. Everyone joined the applause. His face reddened, but he kept juggling. How much time had he spent practicing in order to be able to do this today?

"It can be tricky," Craig said when the room was quiet again. He pretended to almost drop the heart, deftly catching it at the bottom of its arc. "And then children come along." He added a small doll. "It seems like things were a lot easier when you were single and could focus on only one thing at a time."

His eyes found Marlee and she sat up a little straighter and met his searching gaze with one of her own. "There's always the worry you're going to drop something and end up looking like a fool," he said.

The Tin Man sailed out of the arc, falling toward her.

She reached out and caught the small figure, cradling it in both hands. "But then, if you do, you've got someone to catch it and help keep things going," she said.

"That's true." He nodded, continuing to juggle the other objects. "Still, it's a big risk, when you give someone your heart." He stopped abruptly, the items clutched in his hands. He leaned toward her, and offered her the red satin heart.

Her own heart suddenly felt too big for her chest, but somehow she managed to close her fingers around the satin and summon words. "It's a big risk to take it, too."

"I guess it helps if you have the kind of partner who's ready for anything. Someone who's not afraid to strike out in a new direction."

She nodded. "But it's good, too, if one partner is the steady, dependable kind. Someone who plans ahead."

He retrieved the Tin Man from her and started juggling again. "I guess you could say the two balance each other out. Together, they manage better than they would all by themselves."

They looked at each other a long moment, letting their eyes say things they couldn't yet find words for. Marlee's fingers began to ache from gripping the heart so tightly, and her eyes stung from tears she was determined not to let overflow.

After a moment, someone started applauding, and others joined in. Her cheeks felt hot, but she couldn't stop smiling. And she couldn't look away from Craig. She was touched, but still unsure. "I don't know," she said softly. So softly that he had to move closer to hear.

"What don't you know?" he asked, his head close to hers, his voice low so that no one else could hear. Out of the corner of her eye, she saw everyone else begin to drift away.

"I want to believe," she said. "But is it possible? We're so different."

"Not really. Look at all you've done since you've come back from San Diego. You've quit your job and plan to do something better."

"Yeah. I guess I learned a lot on that trip. I didn't want to waste my life anymore."

"I learned a lot, too." He wrapped his hands around hers. "I learned that I don't always have to control everything. I don't have to control you." His eyes met hers, intense and full of meaning. "Give us a chance, Marlee. You said you were open to adventure, so think of our relationship that way—the biggest adventure you could have."

"But what if something goes wrong?"

"Then we'll pick ourselves up and get back on track. Between the two of us we ought to be able to figure a way to make it out, though I don't promise we won't argue about it for a while first."

He smiled and she couldn't help smile in return. A door that had been slammed shut inside her opened wide. "You're stubborn, you know that?"

"I am. Too stubborn to give up on you. On us." He kissed her, a gentle brush of his lips that held the promise of so much more. "I love you, Marlee Jones. You turned my whole life upside down and I ended up liking it. Almost as much as I love you."

"I love you, Craig. I've missed you so much."

"I've missed you, too."

"Does this mean you want me to handle your advertising?"

"At least for the rest of my life."

Her heart fluttered and she swallowed hard. "Let's start with right now and see how it goes from there."

He laughed. "Now who's the cautious one? Okay. No long-term plans—yet. But don't forget I'm a man who likes to think about the future."

"Think about it all you want. As long as we do a good job of dealing with right now."

"We will. Between the two of us we'll manage no matter what detours fate takes us on."

Epilogue

Six months later

"Is the photographer here yet? Is everything ready?"

"He's here. And look at the crowd. They're lined up on the sidewalks, waiting to get in."

"How do I look?"

Marlee turned away from the window and inspected Craig's sparkling white chef's tunic and toque. "You look great. Exactly how the man in charge of the most talked-about new restaurant in the city ought to look."

He glanced over her shoulder at the crowd waiting for the restaurant to open. "Maybe your advertising campaign worked too well."

She turned to the window again. "There's no such thing as a campaign working *too* well." In fact, the campaign she'd designed to promote the new restaurant had garnered enough attention that she had clients clamoring for her services. Her work had never been more fulfilling.

Behind her, Craig moved about the restaurant, straightening a painting here, inspecting silverware there. "Will you settle down?" Mr. Brinkman emerged from the coat check and looked his son up and down. "I didn't raise you to be such a worrywart."

Marlee stifled a smile. She'd persuaded Craig to invite his parents to the grand opening so they could see what a big splash he was making in the city.

"I can't pick up a magazine or newspaper in this town without reading about you or this place," Mr. Brinkman continued. "You're going to have all the business you can handle."

"I still don't quite understand the jugglers." Craig's mother joined them.

"It's part of the whole theme of the restaurant." Marlee pointed out the front window, where a magician and a juggler were entertaining the waiting crowd.

"A theme helps create a buzz, but the real magic is the food," Craig said. "That's what will keep people coming back."

"That beef dish we had last night was certainly good," Mr. Brinkman said. "What did you call it again?"

"Blanketed beef medallions à la Marlee."

Mrs. Brinkman smiled at her. "Do you cook, too, dear?"

She laughed. "Not really, but I've been helping Craig in the kitchen some."

"She's made some very…innovative suggestions for seasonings. Some of which have turned out pretty good."

"And some of them have been awful." She grinned at him. "But hey, you never know unless you take a chance, right?"

"That's our motto." He put his arm around her shoulder. "Come on, let's get things started."

Flashbulbs exploded as soon as they stepped out onto the sidewalk, and some of those waiting burst into applause. They posed behind a swath of blue ribbon, then Craig severed it with a pair of oversize scissors. Then they stepped aside and were officially open for business.

As the hostesses seated their guests, Craig retired to the kitchen and Marlee took her place at the front counter, overseeing it all. She'd helped design not only the ad campaign but the restaurant itself. It was elegant, with black lacquer chairs, smoked glass mirrors and subdued lighting, but there were touches of whimsy in the drama masks on the walls, and magic show props in shadow boxes above each booth.

She smiled at the neon sign in the front window— The Magic Chef. The readers of her blog had suggested the name, and it had been her favorite for purely sentimental reasons. It had taken a little coaxing for Craig to agree, but then, he was growing more sentimental by the day.

She admired the ring on her finger, a yellow diamond in an antique setting they'd found at a vintage store. As Craig had pointed out, no ordinary engagement ring seemed right for her.

She glanced over her shoulder, into the kitchen, where Craig was directing the prep staff and his assistants. He was in his element there, a commander in charge of troops. All business, yet when he looked up and caught sight of her, he grinned.

She winked at him, and blew a kiss. Yes, her life certainly had taken an unexpected turn these days, but it was as she always said in her blog—the best adventures happened when you threw away the map and took a chance in unfamiliar territory.

ATHENA FORCE

The Athena Academy adventure continues....

Three secret sisters
Three super talents
One unthinkable legacy...

The ties that bind may be the ties that kill as these extraordinary women race against time to beat the genetic time bomb that is their birthright....

**Don't miss the latest three stories
in the Athena Force continuity**

DECEIVED by Carla Cassidy, January 2005

CONTACT by Evelyn Vaughn, February 2005

PAYBACK by Harper Allen, March 2005

**And coming in April–June 2005,
the final showdown for
Athena Academy's best and brightest!**

Available at your favorite retail outlet.

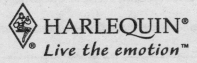

If you enjoyed what you just read,
then we've got an offer you can't resist!

Take 2 bestselling love stories FREE!

Plus get a FREE surprise gift!

Clip this page and mail it to Harlequin Reader Service®

IN U.S.A.
3010 Walden Ave.
P.O. Box 1867
Buffalo, N.Y. 14240-1867

IN CANADA
P.O. Box 609
Fort Erie, Ontario
L2A 5X3

YES! Please send me 2 free Harlequin Flipside™ novels and my free surprise gift. After receiving them, if I don't wish to receive anymore, I can return the shipping statement marked cancel. If I don't cancel, I will receive 2 brand-new novels every month, before they're available in stores! In the U.S.A., bill me at the bargain price of $4.24 plus 50¢ shipping & handling per book and applicable sales tax, if any*. In Canada, bill me at the bargain price of $4.94 plus 50¢ shipping & handling per book and applicable taxes**. That's the complete price—what a great deal! I understand that accepting the 2 free books and gift places me under no obligation ever to buy any books. I can always return a shipment and cancel at any time. Even if I never buy another book from Harlequin, the 2 free books and gift are mine to keep forever.

131 HDN DZ9H
331 HDN DZ9J

Name	(PLEASE PRINT)
Address	Apt.#
City	State/Prov.	Zip/Postal Code

Not valid to current Harlequin Flipside™ subscribers.

Want to try two free books from another series?
Call 1-800-873-8635 or visit www.morefreebooks.com.

* Terms and prices subject to change without notice. Sales tax applicable in N.Y.
** Canadian residents will be charged applicable provincial taxes and GST.
All orders subject to approval. Offer limited to one per household.
® and ™ are registered trademarks owned and used by the trademark owner and or its licensee.

© 2004 Harlequin Enterprises Ltd.

FLIPS04R